# A
# Descent
## INTO
# Darkness

A NEVERLAND CHRONICLES SAGA | PART ONE
# T.S. Kinley

A Decent into Darkness,
A Neverland Chronicles Saga Part One
by T. S. Kinley

First paperback edition January 2024
ISBN 979-8-9859074-8-3

Book design by T.S. Kinley
Editing by Samantha Swart
Cover design by T.S. Kinley
WWW.TSKinleyBooks.com

*For those of you who can't help falling for the villain, this one's for you. In a world of black and white, may you find beauty in the vibrant shades of morally grey.*

# AUTHOR'S NOTE

The content in this book contains sexually explicit depictions. Please be aware of the following possible trigger warnings and read at your own discretion. Lewd NSFW depictions of sexual acts, bondage/restraints, BDSM, blood play, non con, attempted rape, dub con, brief mentions of childhood sexual assault, prostitution, drug and alcohol use, poisoning, graphic violence, hanging, drowning, abduction, assault, guns, swords, hostage situations, mind control, religion, anxiety, depression, death. This book ends in a cliffhanger.

This work of historical fiction is a creative endeavor that blends real historical settings with fictional characters and events. While every effort has been made to capture the essence of the time period and provide an authentic backdrop, it is essential to note that the narrative takes artistic liberties and deviates from historical accuracy. Characters, dialogues, and certain plot elements have been crafted for dramatic effect, cohesion, and entertainment purposes.

*"It is absolutely necessary, for the peace and safety of mankind, that some of earth's dark, dead corners and unplumbed depths be let alone; lest sleeping abnormalities wake to resurgent life, and blasphemously surviving nightmares squirm and splash out of their black lairs to newer and wider conquests."*
—H.P. Lovecraft

# PROLOGUE

## Captain James Hook

### PRESENT DAY

"Life is a hideous thing, and from the background behind what we know of it peer daemoniacal hints of truth which make it sometimes a thousandfold more hideous." H.P. Lovecraft couldn't word it more eloquently. Life is full of hardships and unspeakable pain. Even in your perceived happiest of times. When things seem to be going in your favor. Evil lurks just around the corner, waiting to obliterate your sliver of peace.

I used to think the idea of a happily ever after was a myth. A notion we fragile humans use as a way to keep moving forward, pushing through the pain of everyday life. Searching for that elusive place in time where everything is perfect, and the pain subsides. Truth is, you have to know misery to recognize bliss. Know true hatred to be capable of true love.

I lived countless lifetimes before finding my fabled happy ending. My *Darling* girl, my soul mate, my missing piece. But this isn't the story of our love affair. There won't be a happy ending to this part of the story, because to get to my happily ever after, I first had to become the notorious Captain Hook. This is my story. The story of how I became vilified in the name of revenge.

# CHAPTER ONE
## -BETRAYAL-

### Jas

#### 1703

O ur lives are nothing more than a collection of fickle memories. Weathered footprints lingering on shifting sands, slowly eroding with each passing tide. Their finer details fading like old ink on ancient parchment. A crumbling testament to the beauty and pain of it all, the vibrant colors muted by forgetfulness. But it's the ones that are burned into our minds, the ones branded on our soul, that determine what sort of life we will lead.

The image of that filthy alleyway is one of the very first memories that tattooed itself onto my soul. My eyes burned with the need for sleep, but something in my squirming mind refused to let me rest as it took in every detail of the surrounding squalor. It was a demon that had taken up residence in my soul, clinging to a life that wasn't worth living—And its name was revenge.

I would have gladly welcomed the peaceful oblivion of sleep, never to be awoken again. It would have been the perfect escape from the hell I'd found myself in. But vengeance consumed me, and it ripped away the very notion of taking the easy way out. Instead, I focused on the filth before me. This was the very bottom of the humanity barrel and I wanted to remember every detail. I promised myself I would never forget what I had been reduced to.

Discarded wooden boxes were stacked against cold stone walls, making the narrow passageways almost suffocating. Piles of refuse lay in every corner, each accompanied by a hoard of flies that droned on in an endless buzzing that filled my ears. I cleared my throat quickly, trying to ignore the stench that threatened to gag me. Not that there was anything in my stomach left to lose. The foul stench served to stave off the gnawing hunger pangs, at least for now. I pulled myself upright, wiped the dirt from my face with my sleeve, and slicked my hair back into a frayed scrap of fabric. It was more dirty than blonde at this point and I'd all but given up on bathing.

My mind drifted to Neverland. My traitorous thoughts showed me visions of the paradise that had once been mine. I could be bathing in her pristine lagoons and feasting on the fruits of the isle. But it had been stolen from me. My friend—my *brother*—had taken everything from me. He'd betrayed me, left me to die in this godforsaken place. I let the wrath consume me. I let it fill me until the urge to rise and continue living finally emerged. I lived for him now. I would have my sweet revenge. I would satisfy that ever present itch when I finally killed Peter Pan.

I rose to my feet, stretching out my stiff muscles, wincing as a sharp pain radiated from my shoulder. My hand shot to the festering wound, instinctually covering it until the pain subsided enough for me to pull in a settling breath. It was my final parting gift from Pan. I'd been on the wrong side of his sword for the first time in my life, and the cool metal of his blade had left me with a burning reminder of how much I hated him. I peeked under the ragged cloth I'd used in a futile attempt to keep it bandaged. The skin around the wound was an angry red, and still hadn't healed. Only now, instead of blood, it wept a yellow fluid that added to the sickly smells around me.

Church bells tolled, calling parishioners to start the day. Just my luck, it was a Sunday. The one day everyone else rested, all but guaranteed me work. I was still trying to devise a plan to earn a steady wage, but work had been almost nonexistent for a scrawny, teenaged boy with no experience or family to speak of. But every day was another opportunity to claw my way out of the gutter in which Pan had abandoned me. My stomach pulled me from my brooding, reminding me it had been severely neglected.

Today, I'd spend time at the docks. I'd heard news that ships were expected into the harbor any day now, and maybe I could earn a few shillings unloading cargo. But first, I needed to see to some food. I'd pushed myself as long as I could, but I'd be no help to anyone if I keeled over from starvation. And that bastard Pan would go on living without a second thought of me dead and rotting in the ground.

I started down the cobbled alleyways, hiding amongst the shadows until I reached *The Gilded Filly*. I wrapped my knuckles gently on the back door. It was early, but this place was always open for business. The door opened a slit, revealing only the wide, blue eyes of the new girl, Mary.

"Forgive the early hour, mum, but is your madame in?" I asked, shifting my gaze to my feet as she looked me over.

"You're a bit young, don't you think? Do you even have any coin?"

"I… ahhh—"

"Mary? Who is—?" The door swung open, and Madame Matisse's cunning eyes settled on me. "Oh, Jas, it's only you."

"Begging your pardon, mum, but seeing that it's Sunday and all, I was wondering if I might help with the week's laundry, and maybe you'd allow me some breakfast?" I'd met the madame a week after Pan had marooned me back in our realm. I'd been nearly feral with hunger at the time, and I'd attempted to steal her purse in broad daylight. But a woman doesn't become the mistress of the most lucrative brothel in all of South Carolina without knowing how to handle rowdy men. I'd ended up on the ground, the barrel of her pistol trained right between my eyes. She could have shot me right then and there, but she'd taken in my disheveled state and pity had softened her hard expression. She'd offered many young women a refuge, a home, when they had nowhere else to go. Had I been a lady, I might have been useful to her, and honestly she'd appraised me a few times for whatever dark fetishes her clients might have requested, but all she ever offered me was a hot meal in exchange for good hard labor.

This time was no different. Her gaze softened as she took in the sight of me and let out a deep sigh. "Oh, alright, it was a busy night and one of the maids has taken ill. Hurry up with it, and maybe try to wash up a bit, boy. I don't want your smell lingering on my linens." She waved me into the small dining room tucked away at the back of the house. Several of the regular girls nodded at me in greeting. For a so-called 'house of ill repute,' I found more generosity here with Madame Matisse and her courtesans than anywhere else. The wealthy among the city had turned their noses, ignoring me completely. It was easier to pretend the poor didn't exist than bother with the likes of a gutter rat, like me.

The madame turned in a flurry of skirts and I followed, picking up my pace to keep up, her heeled boots clicking rapidly down a narrow hallway. She motioned me toward the large pile of soiled linens heaped at the bottom of the back stairwell.

"No dilly dallying. They need to be washed and dried before business picks up again tomorrow. Once ya get them hung on the line, go help yourself to whatever is in the kitchen."

I spent the better part of the morning elbow deep in the large wooden tub the madame used to clean the linens. The bedsheets smelled like stale sweat, sex, and alcohol. I cringed when I saw the spots of blood mingled in with the other stains on the fabric. Another example of how despicable our realm was. These women were nothing more than a commodity, forced to choose between a life of degradation or a death from starvation. I was thankful the madame hadn't propositioned me. I think I preferred to take my chances on the streets. I turned my thoughts to Pan. It was easier to let my mind fantasize about the many ways I would have my revenge than to focus on the harsh realities that were right in front of me.

"Jas? Oh, Jas, there ya are," Madame Matisse called to me as she bustled into the tiny courtyard at the back of the house. Her petite face popped out from behind a row of sheets drying on the line. "I've gotten word that one of our most valued clients arrived at port this morning. I have to head to the tavern to secure their finest rum. I need you to go up to Charlotte's room. Let her know *Queen Anne's Revenge* has arrived and she must... prepare herself for our special guest." She hesitated at the end of her request, trying in vain to preserve my delicate sensibilities, as though I was naïve to the going's on at her establishment. But I smiled and nodded politely, trying to hide my blush. Miss Charlotte was the most beautiful woman at *The Gilded Filly,* and the most coveted. I scooped a handful of the cloudy water I'd been using to launder the sheets and splashed my face in a vain attempt to look the least bit respectable before I presented my message to Miss Charlotte. When my eyes popped open, they met an exasperated glare from Madame Matisse.

"Get on with it, lad," she chided, a knowing grin cracking her half-hearted scowl. "There's no time to waste." I nodded again, fumbling over a slew of apologies as I made my way toward the house. Maybe the tides were beginning to turn in my favor. The ships I'd been waiting on had finally arrived.

I stumbled up the back stairwell, tripping over my gangly limbs. I was growing so damn fast; I'd had almost a foot on Pan before he'd abandoned me. Now I could only hope my height and the potential for the man I'd become would be enough to impress Miss Charlotte. When I reached her door, I straightened myself and tried to smooth out my disheveled clothes as best I could before gently knocking.

"Who is it?" The sweetest voice flowed from behind the door.

"Uh— sorry to bother you, milady. But, I— uh…" Every thought in my brain vanished. I stood outside her door like a babbling fool, trying to think of something to say, anything at all, but my very own name eluded me at the moment. I heard rustling behind the door. The creak of the hardware as the knob began to turn had me wringing my hands in nervous anticipation. Candle light flooded into the darkened hallway, setting a blazing halo around the voluptuous blonde standing in the doorway.

"Jas, darling, what are you doing up here?" she asked, placing a hand on her hip as she looked me over with a coy smile, likely an occupational reflex. She was dressed in nothing more than her shift, and the gauzy white cotton clung to her breasts and hugged her rounded hips, leaving little to the imagination. My throat went dry instantly, but I managed to fumble through a few more words.

"Sorry to… to trouble you, Miss Charlotte, but—"

"You're no trouble at all. Actually, I could use your help. Come in." She reached out and grabbed my hand, pulling me forward and into the small room she used to entertain half the men in Charles Town. "I was thinking about moving the bed closer to the window. Thought I might fancy the view, and the breeze from the harbor is quite nice in the heat of summer. Do you think you could arrange it for me?"

She stood too close. Her delicate fingers lingered on my arm, scorching the skin beneath. I'd never been this close to a woman. At least not one that made my mind whirl with impure thoughts. It had been my interest in the beautiful nymphs back in Neverland that had further exposed my secret. Not only had my body been changing, but my mind had begun to lust after things only a man would desire. As much as I'd tried to hide it, Pan had figured it out. I broke his cardinal rule.

*Never, ever grow up.*

And yet I couldn't prevent it, no matter how hard I wished it to be so.

I swallowed hard, taking a step back from the seductive

temptress. Thoughts of Pan helped to pull my wayward mind back into the present.

"I'd be happy to help you, mistress, but Madame Mat—"

"You really are filling out, aren't you?"

"Well, yes, I—"

"Have you ever been with a woman before?"

"Umm, well, yes—I mean, no. What do you mean by 'with a woman?' I'm here with you—a woman—right now." She laughed, the sound like sweet bells in my ear and in that moment she looked like a pixie in human form. She closed the small gap between us, pressing her large breasts against my chest. I wondered if she could feel my heart pounding away just beneath the surface.

"You are too sweet. Maybe I could take away some of that sweetness. I might be willing to take on a charity case. Show you how to treat a woman," she purred.

"That's awfully kind of you, mistress. But Madame Matisse sent me with an urgent message. I was to tell you *Queen Anne's Revenge* has arrived at port."

Charlotte's eyes widened as the news finally broke through her seduction, and her demeanor changed instantly.

"What else did she say?" Her voice quavered for a moment as she grabbed a fist full of my shirt.

"That you were to prepare yourself."

"Jesus, Mary, and Joseph, he's returned early this season," she mused to herself. "Did she say when?"

"No mistress, just that I was to come straight away." A

flash of fear flitted across her beautiful eyes before she started pushing me toward the door.

"Off with you. He mustn't find you here, or else—" Her words were cut short by the sound of heavy boots echoing in the stairwell. Charlotte froze, her fingernails biting into my arm as she clung to me. We both stood motionless, silently waiting to see if the stranger in the hallway would simply pass us by. Charlotte jumped when a heavy fist pounded on the door, the solid wood trembling with the force. A thick silence hung in the air for what seemed like an eternity. Charlotte's hand trembled as the color drained from her features.

"Let me in, sweetness. I know you're in there," a deep, graveled voice rumbled through the closed door.

"Jas," she whispered, "you have to hide. Get under the bed. Stay there until I tell you to. Don't come out, no matter what you hear." She knelt down on the floor, coaxing me to follow her, her eyes pleading with me to do as she said. The door rattled again, the banging becoming urgent. "Please, if you won't do it for yourself, do it for me!" The look in her eyes, the frantic tone of her voice, had my heart pounding, this time from the fear that radiated off her. My head bobbled in a shaky nod, and I scrambled under the bed. The lace fell into place just as Charlotte opened the door.

# CHAPTER TWO

## -HOPE-

### *Jas*

H is leather boots were worn and weathered, and they clunked ominously as he crossed the floor, stopping mere feet from my shrouded face.

"Edward," Charlotte spoke his name as if the word itself brought promise of sinful pleasures. "Your back early this season."

"I'm not here for small talk. I'm here to get my cock wet."

"We both know you're here for more than that," she cooed.

"Not today, Charlotte. I'm only in port for a breath. I'll be gone before tomorrow breaks light. Now, why aren't you on your knees?" His words were short and demanding, and Charlotte wasted no time dropping to the floor.

I had often spied on the fae having sex back in Neverland. It wasn't hard to do. They were a wanton people who didn't care much for modesty. But I had never been this close to humans doing it. Curiosity piqued my interest, and I watched through the lacy windows of light. Edward's pants fell around his ankles, exposing his dirty, hairy legs, while Charlotte kneeled in front of him. I wriggled closer to the lace concealing my hiding place, trying to see above his knees, but they were too far away. I could hear his excitement. He was groaning loudly, while Charlotte, on the other hand, was gagging and gasping for air. Did she like that? Was that normal? Fear had me paralyzed. Was he trying to kill her? I began to panic. If Charlotte died while I stayed silently under the bed, Madame Matisse would have my hide for sure. Charlotte had said to stay hidden no matter what I saw or heard. But this was nothing like I had seen in Neverland. I was about to expose myself in a chivalrous attempt to rescue my damsel in distress when Edward pulled her up from the floor and dropped her shift in a puddle at her feet.

"My dirty little whore likes it rough, doesn't she?"

"Aye, My Captain," Charlotte's voice was full of lust. "Use me for your pleasure."

I held my breath. Fearful he would hear my rapid

breathing. Charlotte gasped before he pushed her back on to the bed.

"Play with your pussy while I take off my boots. I wanna see how wet you are for me." His words were vulgar and yet they stirred a need within my pants. I wanted desperately to see what was happening but all I could manage from this position was a silhouetted reflection against the wall, flickering in the candle light. Charlotte's knees were bent, and she was leaning back. Her hands busy between her parted legs and soft moans escaped her lips. His boots hit the floor in a series of loud thuds. One after the other startling me from my locked gaze, moments before his pants dropped directly in front of my face, obscuring my view.

The bed groaned with his added weight pulling on the ropes supporting the stained mattress above me. The sounds of their escapades quickly filled the space. Making me uncomfortably aware of the predicament I found myself in. Hopefully, he would make quick work of his needs with Charlotte, and I could get back to my chores.

While the two of them were distracted with each other, I seized the opportunity to rifle through the man's pockets. A handful of Spanish dollars, an old and weathered compass, and to my surprise, a small vial of golden sparkling dust. *Could it be?*

My heart started to pound in my chest. I rolled the vial between my fingers. Watching as the contents glimmered in the dim light. I never thought I'd see it again. I quickly opened the vial, said a prayer to the Divine, and smeared a bit of the dust across my now oozing wound. I winced as the pain flared. A smile spread across my face as I watched my shoulder mend itself. The pain instantly subsided. It was indeed faerie dust.

This was it. My way back home—back to Neverland. A chance at sweet revenge. I had to find a way to befriend this Edward. He was obviously more than your ordinary sailor, or was it a façade to hide his true nature? I needed to figure out exactly who or what he was, and what he knew of the other realms. Find out how he got his hands on faerie dust. Surely he had valuable connections. Connections that could lead to Neverland. If I was going to get back, I was going to need a lot more than this small vial. I stuffed the money back into his pants and rolled the vial of dust once more between my fingers. I couldn't bring myself to put it back. What if I couldn't find more? I pocketed the vial and the compass. If I played my cards right, I might be able to use the compass as a way to get an audience with Edward. For the first time since being dropped on the unfamiliar streets of Charles Town, I had a glimmer of hope. This would be my ticket home.

EDWARD KEPT Charlotte busy for the better part of an hour before he finally left the room. I scrambled out from under the bed, ignoring Charlotte's laughter. She must have thought I was scarred from the experience. But I no longer cared what she thought of me. My mind was solely focused on one thing. I needed to get to Edward. I followed him quietly down to the common room, slinking along the walls so as not to be seen.

For a Sunday afternoon, *The Gilded Filly* was bustling with patrons. Several of the girls were entertaining potential clients, hoping to seduce them out of their coin. Others simply enjoyed a voyeuristic drink. I lingered in the shadowed corners, silently watching as Madame Matisse offered the captain her finest bottle of rum. He sat at the bar alone, forgoing the glass and drinking straight from the bottle. He was a large man. Considerably taller than me with a full beard of black hair. His wild eyes were intense, almost sinister in their appearance. This was my moment. It was now or never. I had heard him tell Charlotte he would be gone before day's end. Time was fleeting. I had to get it right.

"Mr. Edward," I mumbled. Catching his attention was intimidating, to say the least, but I needed faerie dust, and this man had a connection.

"Edward," I said it with confidence this time. He turned to face me.

"What do you want? I'm not interested in fornicating with a young man."

Young man. His words hit a nerve. Reminding me of the pain Peter had inflicted for the inescapable sin of growing up. No matter how hard I'd wished, I was powerless to stop the march of time. And yet, Pan had punished me anyway. All for something I couldn't control. Man... it was a simple word, and yet it stoked the rage boiling deep within me.

I took a cleansing breath. I wouldn't allow my anger to

get in the way of this opportunity. I pulled the compass from my pocket. "I believe this belongs to you, sir."

His brow furrowed as confusion set in. "Where did you get that?" He reached for the compass, and I quickly retracted my hand.

"I found it outside of Miss Charlotte's room. She told me you were leaving before daybreak. I— I…"

"Out with it, boy. I haven't got all day."

"I would like to join your crew." The words just blurted out. "The compass for a position on your ship. I'll prove myself worthy, sir. I'm a hard worker."

He pondered my offer, taking a long pull off the bottle of rum. I took the slight hint of amusement on his face as a good sign. "A brave soul you are trying to barter your way on to my ship using my own belongings. Tell me, what exactly makes you valuable to my crew?"

"I'm willing to do anything. Please, just give me a chance."

He sighed and took another pull from the bottle. "You're in luck. As it were, I need a new powder monkey." He reached up stroking his full black beard. "The last one got careless with the gunpowder and found himself burnt to a crisp."

"Yes, a powder monkey! I'll be the best powder monkey you've ever had." I had no idea what a powder monkey was. I didn't care as long as it got me on Edward's ship.

"Get your ass down to the docks before sundown. Don't be late. I won't wait for you. Now, I'll take my compass back. What's your name, young man?"

James, sir. My name is James, but you can call me Jas. Thank you. I won't disappoint you." I handed him back the old compass.

"It's Captain. If I catch you stealing from me again, I won't think twice about cutting off your hands. Do you understand, Jas?"

"Yes, Captain." I had no idea who this man was or just how dangerous he might be, but my options were limited. I could stay here in Charles Town and hope for another vial of faerie dust to fall into my lap or I could take my chances with this mysterious stranger who harbored secrets that might just get me back to Neverland. The choice was simple. I was off to sea.

# CHAPTER THREE
## -WORTHY-

### Jas

### 1709

**M**y head hung heavy as I waited for my fate. Distracting myself with the minute details of the weathered decking beneath my feet. I'd gotten myself into this position. There was no use regretting it now. I sank into my bindings, enjoying the sting from my wrists. The pain meant I was still alive. I was bound to the foremast above my head. Just enough so my feet barely grazed the wooden planks and my body swayed with the roll of the ship. I heard the crack of the whip before the bite of it radiated across my back. As much as I tried to hold it in, the shock of it pulled a groan from my lips. The warm, wet trickle told me he'd drawn blood this time.

"Nothings better than the scent of blood on the sea air, ain't that right, boys!" Captain called to the crew that had gathered to watch the spectacle. I had learned long ago that Edward Teach had a soul as dark as the devil himself. He had insisted on completing my initiation personally, and he had been vicious in his execution. The moment he declared I would take over as bo'sun on the ship, the torment had commenced. I had to prove myself worthy of the rank. Show my unwavering loyalty to Teach by subjecting myself to torture and degradation.

The last two weeks had been hell. The rigors of pirate life were never easy, but I'd grown accustomed to the grueling labor, and found some solace in it. It helped to swage the vengeful demon that lived within me, impatiently waiting for my chance to return to Neverland. But this was different. Teach had taken great pleasure in my suffering. It had been nothing more than entertainment for his sick, twisted mind.

Tonight, it would all end, one way or another. Either I'd prove my worth or die in the process. I tried to remind myself that I was resilient. The constant work had hardened my body. Pirate life had hardened my soul. Now I was a formidable match for anyone on the ship. All the more reason for Teach to break me.

I'd spent the duration of the initiation on the brink of starvation, granted nothing more than a handful of molded scraps to eat. My hands and feet had been shackled and I'd been forced to work from sunup to sundown. He'd stripped away the very clothes on my back, subjecting my skin to the unrelenting sun. The lingering burn intensified the stinging pain from the lashes on my back.

"How goes it, Jas? You yield?" his graveled voice growled in my ear, the scent of rum thick on his breath.

"May I have another, Captain?" My voice quavered as my body screamed with the pain. It was my will alone that forced the words from my lips even while my soul wept at the idea of the whip across my sensitive flesh.

"We'll make a fine bo'sun out of you yet, my boy." His words were punctuated with another lash from his whip. My whole body tensed as the pain gripped me. This time, I'd been able to stifle the sob that lingered at the back of my throat. That fucker was enjoying every minute of this. I could easily picture the smug smile on his face as he attempted to take me down a peg. I had to remind myself that fate had led me here for a reason. This was the path the Divine had set me on.

"Cut him down, and clean up this mess. Only one thing left to seal the deal, Jas. And then we shall feast."

The young cabin boy scurried into the rigging to cut my bindings. The weight of my body was too much in my weakened state, and I collapsed on the deck in a slippery puddle of my own blood.

*Shit.*

I had to get to my feet. I couldn't show weakness. Not in front of this man. I felt a firm hand on my shoulder. It was

Henry who'd braved Teach's wrath and stepped up to help me to my feet. The roar of a single gunshot pierced my ears, sending a wave of adrenaline pumping through my veins.

"Nobody touches him! He gets to his feet on his own, or he'll rot on the deck with a bullet hole in the back of his head."

Teach loomed over me, his pistol still aimed at the sky, smoke rolling from the barrel. I shrugged Henry's hand from my shoulder, lest he end up with a few matching lashes of his own. He was about the only honorable man on the ship, and I wasn't about to let him suffer for the likes of me. My body was spent, but the drive that burned deep within me refused to give up, and I managed to scramble to my feet on shaky legs.

"Are you ready to pledge the oath now?"

I grunted my agreement.

"Alright, boys, hold him tight," Teach called to the surrounding crew. The moment the order was dropped, they descended on me, grabbing my limbs, pulling at my hair until I was completely immobilized. Teach grabbed a hold of my right wrist, binding it with a rope, the coarse fibers digging into the wounds already present. He pulled my arm tight, stretching it until I felt like my shoulder might pop out of its socket. When he was satisfied, he handed the rope off to his first mate, a vile man they called Drake.

"Can't have you moving, now can we?" Teach chuckled to himself, before pulling a ring from his finger. "You see this?" he asked, holding the heavy ring in front of my face. Its polished silver glinted in the setting sun, catching on a raised skull and crossbones at the center. "This is my mark," he swiped his hand away, palming the ring in a white knuckled grip, "and once it's imbedded in your skin, you're mine." He took a step toward me, his imposing figure still several inches taller than I was, and I had to tilt my chin up to look him in the eye. He studied me for a moment, and it was almost as though I could feel him probing into my soul. "And if you ever cross me... May Manann, the mighty god of the sea, find you before I do." He drew out each word, ensuring that I captured the gravity of what he said. An impossible heat radiated from his hand, the one still clutching the ring, but I couldn't break his stare to see what was happening.

"So what'll it be, Jas? Do you vow fealty to me as your captain?"

"Yes, Captain," I forced the words from my throat and braced myself.

"I was hoping you'd say that." He broke my gaze and focused on my right forearm, the ring reappearing in his fingers, only it glowed red like a hot ember that had just been fished from the fire. Before I could ponder the curiousness of how he'd heated the metal with the only fire being in the galley below deck, he planted the scalding ring on my forearm. A deep, visceral scream bubbled up from my lungs and broke free of my lips as my skin melted beneath the metal of his ring. The pain radiated from my arm, and it felt like my whole body was being charred in the pits of hell. I could feel the bond between Teach and I fuse into my bones, as if some arcane magic had bound my very soul to his.

Teach pulled the ring from my skin, the smell of burnt flesh thick in my nostrils. He examined it briefly, the ring now returned to a polished silver, and placed it on his finger again. I tried in vain to slow my breathing. It was fear that gripped me, rather than the pain. Had I just sold my soul to the devil... or something even worse?

"You've done good, Jas. Boys, show some respect for your bo'sun! Get the man a drink. Now we celebrate."

I WAS USHERED to my new cabin. Each of the crew taking turns to clap my shoulders as they acknowledged my new status. I didn't let it go to my head. Most of them would slit my throat if it meant a raise in ranks. But I couldn't blame them. That's exactly how I'd gotten the promotion myself. When the latch clicked behind me, I took in the space that was now my private quarters. A room that was mine alone, with an actual bed that appeared long enough to fit my tall form. A notable perk of my new position, and a decided upgrade from the hammock I'd had in the main cabin with the rest of the crew. Steam rose from a washbasin that had been set upon the small desk in the corner. There, laid out on the bed, was a neatly folded coat in a rich navy blue with gold details. A fresh pair of twill breeches and a stark white linen shirt. A pair of well-oiled boots had been placed at the foot of the bed with a new belt coiled around them. I'd never had such fine clothes before. I ran my fingers over the coat, finding a note slipped into the breast pocket.

*I had full faith that you'd earn a place of honor amongst my men. A prodigy in the making. Now clean up, get dressed, and meet me on the castle deck. It is time to celebrate. We have much to discuss.*

NOW THAT I'D been brought into Teach's inner circle, I could start probing him for answers. My inner demon squirmed with the possibilities. Ever since that day at *The Gilded Filly*, I'd known Teach was more than he presented to be. I wasn't sure what that was, but I knew he wasn't human. I'd bet my life on it. The way he'd taken a seemingly ordinary ring and used it to burn my flesh without so much as a fire to heat it, only further confirmed my suspicions. I'd been patient. The vengeance within me maturing like a fine wine. I would be a nightmare realized when I finally unleashed this well-honed fury on Pan. Today, I felt closer to realizing that dream than ever before.

SOLID GROUND beneath my new boots was a welcomed reprieve from the sea. My initiation, or rather the two weeks of hell Teach had subjected me to, had been perfectly planned to coincide with our arrival at port. As much as it pained Teach, the deep heat of summer had brought on a particularly nasty storm season, and we'd been forced to return to South Carolina. It couldn't have come at a better time. The ship was overrun with the spoils of victory and the men had begun to grow restless. It was a volatile combination. Simple-minded men with unfathomable wealth at their fingertips and nothing to show for their efforts. But Teach was a smart man. He knew how to push the men to the edge of madness before manipulating them with his perceived generosity.

"To loyalty." Teach held up his glass of rum, a smirk tugging at his bearded face. I gave him a weary glance, my shoulders hunched over the table we shared, and I made no move to clink glasses with him. My whole body ached from the torment I'd endured, and the darkness inside me was spiteful. I wanted something in return, some penance from him for the lengths he'd gone to in order to procure my loyalty. "Come on, boy. It's time to celebrate. And as I figure it, you owe me."

"Owe you?" The words broke through the brooding silence I'd been holding on to. "How did you come to that conclusion?"

"You were little more than a sack of useless bones when I found you. You would have been dead in a fortnight if I hadn't taken your pathetic little deal. Look at you now. I'd say I've raised a damn fine man from the worthless boy that you were."

"I made my fate happen, not you. If you think the countless days of grueling work, the murdering... the unspeakable evils that happen to a young boy on a ship full of heathens in the darkness, somehow makes you a father figure to me—"

"Yes!" he barked at me with indignation in his voice. "The world isn't soft, and soft men get eaten alive. I made you into a weapon. I've seen the notches you carve above your hammock. Each tick of the wood is a debt owed to me. Each life taken means you lived another day. And I'm the one who gave you the skills to accomplish it." He waited for me to respond. To deny the truth of his words, but I couldn't. "That is what you really wanted, isn't it? To become a killer?" He continued, "You think I haven't seen the look in your eye? I know a man hell bent on revenge, and it's been simmering inside you since the moment I laid eyes on your scrawny form."

"You don't know anything about me," I barked at him. I'd gone to great lengths to keep my personal vendettas with Pan a secret. Not that anyone would believe that I'd traveled between worlds and lived for a time amongst the fae.

Teach laughed, slamming his glass of rum on the table, the spiced alcohol splashing the both of us. "Another lesson for you, Jas. Don't underestimate anyone... ever. I know you've seen things, been places you can't explain. I know you understand the world is more than just what's on the horizon before us. And only I can deliver to you what you desire the most. Show some fucking respect. Hold up your glass and toast to the future I'm offering you."

A part of me hated Edward Teach down to the marrow of my bones. The man had left his own black mark on my soul. But he was a necessary evil and without him, I never would have gotten this far. It was time to fully embrace what he was offering.

"It's not Jas anymore. That wretched boy dies today. It's James," I spat at him. Jas was too weak to do the truly dark things required to exact my revenge, but the new man emerging from his ashes was more than capable.

This time I raised my glass. The delicate clink as we toasted the future rang in my ears, despite the boisterous crowd around us. I shot back the rum. The comforting burn coated my throat before he could even get his glass to his lips.

"Good, good! Tomorrow we plan, but tonight is on me. I'm proud of how far you've come."

IT DIDN'T TAKE LONG for the rum to ease my pain and loosen my inhibitions. The food and drinks kept coming all night as Teach told wild tales about sirens and krakens. I tried to hold on to the details, because I knew there was likely some truth to his stories, but the rum clouded everything in a drunken haze, and at that moment I didn't care. My soul felt light. It was the first time in weeks that I had a full belly, and I was numb to my pain. It was almost blissful. By the time Teach and I made it to *The Gilded Filly*, I was stumbling over myself and singing a bawdy tune.

"Why if it ain't Mr. Jas!" A familiar voice called to me as I entered, and Madam Matisse greeted me warmly. The cunning lady of the manor had a few more wrinkles and her dark hair was streaked in grey, but her eyes were just as fierce. "You've grown into a fine man indeed."

"See, James. That's what I've been trying to tell you. I've done right by you," Teach boasted. I grunted my approval, afraid of what might come out of my mouth in my drunken stupor.

"Do you have the room prepared, like I asked?" Teach questioned.

"Aye, sir. First door on your left." She nodded at the captain, and before my mind could catch up, Teach was helping me up the stairs.

"What are we doing?" I managed to mumble the question.

"I'm making sure you've got all the comforts a man could need."

When he opened the door, I was welcomed by the glow of warm candlelight and two beautiful women. Each of them wearing nothing but a string of pearls draped over their ample breasts. They both smiled at me with hungry eyes. Twirling their fingers through the neat ringlets in their hair. One blonde, one brunette.

"What is… what's happening here?" I asked. My throat going dry as my eyes darted between the two of them.

"They're for you, my friend."

"For me? What am I supposed to—" Teach's laugh cut off my question, and he patted my shoulder before seeing himself out and closing the door.

"Hello, James," the blonde called to me. My heart pounded in my chest, burning off the alcohol and sobering me up a bit.

"Why don't cha come over to the bed and let us take care of you," the brunette cooed, motioning me forward. My cock twitched in my pants. I'd had intimacy forced upon me. A dark stain on my brain that rooted its way into my dreams, turning them into nightmares. A young boy on a long voyage learns very quickly to stay hidden from the darkness lurking in the shadows. But instead of the nightmares rearing their ugly heads, my body reacted instinctively. Maybe it was the fact that this was on my terms, or maybe it was the alcohol, but I was now a starved man craving only what these women could offer. I hadn't had much time for women in my life. Hadn't spent more than a few days on shore at any given time and my focus had solely been on earning my way into Teach's good graces. So I'd kept my baser needs in check with the help of my right hand.

Now I realized how inadequate that had been. I wanted more. I'd earned this night. I walked to the bed, the brunette stepping toward me, unbuttoning my shirt, while the blond stepped to my back and helped me out of it. They smelled sweet, like violets in summer. My eyes lingered on the curves of their bodies, entranced by the fairer sex as they unbuckled my belt and slipped my breeches down.

The brunette reached up on her tiptoes to kiss me. My cock pressed against her belly, rock hard between the two of us. Her delicate fingers traced along my jaw, weaving into my hair, deepening the kiss until her tongue was exploring mine. My hands fell to her full breasts, reveling at how soft they felt in my palm. I'd never touched a woman in such an intimate way before. My mind was an erratic mess. Pulled between the brunette in front of me, and the blonde trailing kisses down my ruined back. My body melted into them, I felt nails dragging across my back, leaving a trail of burning fire behind them.

"Ahh," I sucked in a deep breath through clenched teeth.

"Do ya want us to stop?" the blonde asked with a mocking coyness.

"No, don't stop," I breathed.

My darkness purred. The combination of such intense sensations was a heady mix. Pain and pleasure mixed together like a brewing tempest. Thunder and lightning colliding and the fury of the storm was unleashed within me. I turned to the blonde, claiming her smart mouth with a punishing kiss. My teeth sunk into her lip until I tasted the metallic tang of blood, and I devoured her moan with another kiss. She pushed me back toward the bed. When the back of my legs felt the mattress, she gave me a hard shove and I let myself fall onto the bed.

The brunette descended on me, straddling my chest, kissing and nipping her way downward. While the blonde tied my hands to the metal bedposts with silk ropes. Before I could protest, I felt soft lips engulf the head of my cock. The warm, wet sensation of her tongue as it swirled over the tip was enough to make my toes curl. I couldn't care less if they wanted to chain me to their bed and never let me leave.

My eyes were locked on the chocolate curls as she bobbed up and down, gagging on my length until I was thrusting to meet her with every stroke. Just when I thought I'd spill my seed down her throat, the blonde caught my attention again. She held a candle in her hand, the flame dancing in my eyes before she turned it on its side, pouring a cascade of burning wax onto my chest. The stinging burn added a whole new edge to the pleasure, driving it to another level. The brunette pulled away from me, the subtle breeze felt cool on my heated skin. The blonde quickly took her place. Only instead of her mouth, she rubbed her sex over me, coating me in her arousal.

"Fuck!" The word slipped out in a growl. I waited with bated breath until she sunk herself down on my rigid length, the feel of her erasing the last several weeks. Her features softened in the heat of pleasure. The brunette was eager to join us, and pulled her friend into a lustful kiss. The spectacle threatening to send me over the edge.

*Clove Hitch.*

*Figure Eight.*

*Carrick Bend.*

*Overhand Knot.*

I began mentally reciting sailing knots and picturing them in my head. Desperate to think of anything besides the pair before me. I didn't want it to be over. Not yet.

"Your captain told us you've been bad, and that you deserved to be punished," the brunette purred before pulling a leather flogger from the bedside table. This completely derailed me, pulling my attention away from the list of knots and the blonde riding my cock. The sight of any sort of whip should have chilled me to the bone after what had happened to me earlier. But the tasseled leather from the flogger in her hands made my mind burn with desire.

"Oh yes, I've been bad. Positively filthy, milady," I growled at her, desperate for the punishment she promised. When the sting of the tassels caressed my chest, I was done for. My cock swelled with each strike of the flogger. My balls drawing in as the symphony of pain and pleasure ravaged me. I came with a feral growl. Filling the blonde with my seed in the most intense high. When I finally came back down to my body, both girls draped over my chest, I knew I'd never be the same. I was broken, never to be whole again. I craved this darkness. I would seek out this line between pain and pleasure and see how far I could push it.

# CHAPTER FOUR
## -ACCUSED-

### James

I sucked in a deep breath, my body jolting into consciousness. Muffled shouting had snatched me out of a dreamless sleep and now my heart pounded in my chest while my mind played catch up. A soft coo and the shift of a body beside me brought reality crashing back. The two girls from the previous night were tucked into my side, a spray of hair covering their faces, a tangle of blonde and brunette. My mind began to replay visions of the night's activities and my cock twitched against the sheets.

But just when my thoughts were about to take a devious

turn, the shouting returned, filtering up from the streets below. I gently removed myself from the girls. Their moans of protest had me cursing my curiosity. I should have stayed in bed and indulged in them again, but something nagged at me, luring me from the comforts of the bed.

Rays of sunlight streamed in through the window. I'd slept late. I couldn't remember the last time I'd slept past the dawn. I hopped into my breeches as I made my way to the small window that overlooked the main street below. The road was filled with people, all of them bustling about, straining to see something that was just out of my view.

"Do either of you know what's going on down there?" I called to the girls who were still spread out on the bed covered in nothing more than last night's soiled sheets.

"Aye, today's the trial for that poor orphan girl. The whole town's been a buzz with the news." The blonde answered with a yawn, looking more interested in returning to sleep than the obvious commotion going on in town.

"Since when does a lowly orphan girl garner so much attention? Looks like the entire towns in the streets."

"That's because she's been charged with a capital crime." I turned my attention from the window and cocked an eyebrow at the girl in the bed, my interest thoroughly piqued.

"They say she's a *witch*," she whispered the words as if God himself were listening in.

"A witch?" I repeated skeptically. Real magic was almost nonexistent in this realm. The accusation of witch was usually nothing more than an easy death sentence for those that didn't conform to society.

"It was Jeremiah Grant, the governor's nephew, ya see," she explained, her face becoming animated as she relayed the town gossip. "They say she cast a spell on him. Cursed the bastard to die a horrible death. That she poisoned his mortal soul. But if ya ask me," she lowered her voice again to a whisper, "he deserved whatever he got. The devil may have sent a witch to do his dirty work, but I think God was happy to send that man to the pits of hell." The scarred look on her face told me she knew firsthand of the evils the man had been capable of. "And now the governor is out for blood. Everyone knows today's trial's a farce. She'll be burnin' at the stake by daybreak tomorrow."

I was entranced by the story. Maybe there was more to the girl than meets the eye. Could she be a fae in hiding? I had to get a better look. Not that the fae were easy to identify. Hell, I was still speculating whether or not Teach was fae, and I'd lived in close quarters with the man for years. My gaze reverted to the window, the crowd growing frenzied as a group of men pushed through, dragging a bound woman behind them. Her shackled wrists pulled her petite form forward, causing her to stumble in a vain attempt to keep up with her captors. Waves of blonde hair fell into her face, blocking me from seeing her clearly. Her clothes were filthy and threadbare, with several holes among the mud caked skirts.

"Make way! Coming through!" the men called, pushing

through the crowd as they hurled rotten food and called derogatory names at the woman as she passed. None of it seemed to affect her. Her gaze was focused on the ground, and it drove me crazy that I couldn't see her face. Something about her, the way she carried herself. Not at all like a young woman being led to her death. I needed to get closer. I needed to talk to her. If she was indeed a fae in hiding, I could offer my assistance in exchange for a favor. At this point, I was desperate to get back to Neverland. It had taken years to get close to Teach with no guarantee that he could actually get me there. I had to keep myself open to other options. No lead was too small to follow up on. Every day Peter Pan went on living without paying for his crimes against me was a day too long. I felt the demon flex in my chest. My vengeance was tired of waiting.

I pulled a few coins from my belt. "Thanks for last night. It was quite memorable." I nodded at them, setting the tip on the bedside table, and grabbing the rest of my things.

I had to find Teach. See if he knew anything about this trial that seemed to grip the entire town. I found him lounging in the parlor, a voluptuous redhead sitting in his lap.

"James," he called. A big grin spreading across his face. "You look well. A woman's touch always does the trick. Are you ready—"

"Do you know what's going on in town? The trial, I mean."

Teach plucked the woman from his lap, getting to his feet.

All traces of the grin gone from his face. "Day one as my bo'sun and already you're talking over me. Don't forget your place. You live to serve me, not whatever whim takes your fancy."

I took a step back, dropping my gaze from his cunning eyes. I'd learned to take orders at an early age, but it wasn't something that came naturally. I knew my own mind, I had my own agenda, but I had to remind myself that my liberties were a temporary sacrifice to accomplish my ultimate goal. "I beg your pardon, Captain."

"Ah, James, at ease, my boy. A taste of power always leaves you wanting more. It's how you curb that hunger, only indulging at the proper time. That's how real power is gained," he said, clapping my shoulder. "Now, I have an important meeting to see to. I need you to take charge of the repairs while we're at port. Get the cargo unloaded and be sure to post the most reliable amongst the crew to stand guard. I've arranged a meeting for you with one of the governor's lackeys at noon. You're to collect a payment, but you'll only accept gold and silver. I'll not take any bills of credit. I want to be out of this godforsaken town by the week's end. We'll ride out the rest of the storm season in New Providence."

I almost laughed. We'd been at port less than twenty-four hours and his skin was already crawling with the need to leave. The *Queen Anne* never stayed anchored for long. Teach was always searching, questing for something, and it wasn't more riches. No matter how many ships we took, he was never satisfied. Seeing that I'd already gotten under his skin, I thought it in my best interest not to rile the man by questioning him on his neurotic behavior.

"Might I ask who you'll be meeting?"

"You can ask, but you've not gotten into my good graces enough to earn a response. Now off with ya. The day is wasting away."

"Aye, sir. And when should I expect you back?" It was a common question for the captain. But I hoped he couldn't see through the façade. I needed to know how much time I had to complete my tasks and still look into the girl behind his back.

"I'll be gone all day. Plan to meet me at the pub around seven o'clock. Take inventory of everything and we'll discuss what rations we need to procure before heading to Nassau."

I nodded briefly before turning on my heels. Teach was a master at reading people, and I couldn't allow him to see the deceit flare in my eyes.

THE SUN HAD ALREADY SUNK below its zenith when I finally managed to get through the double doors at the back of the courthouse. It was the finest building in the city, and it was filled beyond capacity. I'd had to use my size and the intensity of my glare to worm my way through the crowd. It hadn't been pretty, but I'd gotten all of my responsibilities taken care of in record time before rushing into town. I'd pushed the crew hard—harder than the bo'sun before me—but I had to establish myself.

"Not sure what you're playing at, James," Henry said with a cautionary tone.

"They have to know that I expect the best," I explained.

"Why do I get the feeling there is more to the story here?" he speculated.

"You and your damn intuition. It's going to get you killed someday," I joked. "But you'll cover for me tonight, yeah?" I met his gaze with sincerity this time. He huffed and rolled his eyes.

"I hope you know what you're doing," he conceded, and I slapped him on the shoulder in appreciation. Henry was the only man on the ship whose opinion mattered to me and the only man I trusted to have my back.

The crew had cursed my name all day until they received a generous stipend for the night. Not only did it get me back into their good graces, but the extra money meant the alcohol would be flowing and no one would notice my absence.

But all my efforts had been in vain. The moment I entered the room, an authoritative voice was calling over the din of the crowd.

"After hearing testimony in the case against Katherine Elizabeth Hawkins, we hereby find the accused guilty of the murder of Jeremiah Michael Collins by way of witchcraft. As God's loyal servants, we cannot allow a witch to live. I, therefore, sentence Miss Hawkins to death." The entire crowd burst into nervous chatter. The sharp pounding of a gavel echoed over the room. "Order! I'll have order in this court!" The judge rose from his bench, his neatly powdered wig appearing at odds with the dark scowl on his wrinkled face.

My eyes darted to the woman at the center of it all. Her back was to me, but as before, her gaze remained solidly on the ground at her feet. She made no effort to defend herself, no wailing or crying. Her body was perfectly still, not even the tell-tale shaking of silent sobbing. My heart raced in my chest. I needed to know more about this woman who faced certain death with such admirable stoicism.

A plan took shape in my mind. A long shot with too many variables to consider, but it was all I could think of in that moment. I said a little prayer to the Divine that fate was on my side as I pulled my flask from my pocket and took a hearty swig of rum. The alcohol burned my throat before settling in my belly. The rest of the contents I poured over my clothes, dousing myself with the potent cologne that would ensure my plan would work. I waited for the final judgment. When the crowd settled, the judge returned to his seat.

"The accused shall be remanded into custody and come morning, she shall burn at the pyre for her crimes against God."

This was my cue. I instantly became animated, throwing my large frame into the crowd. "A witch?" I questioned, raising my voice so it echoed in the momentary quiet of the chamber. "Or a fae? Only the Divine can know for sure!" I purposefully slurred the words, putting on a show as I stumbled through the throng of bystanders. I needed to make a scene. The crowd began to protest as I continued to ramble incoherent words, flailing about as though I'd been overcome with the drink. Public drunkenness was still against the law, even though most of the time it was simply ignored. But the publicity of this trial was too important for my actions to go unnoticed. I continued pushing forward, desperate to get a glimpse of the girl. My actions roused the crowd, drawing all the attention solely on me. It was then that she finally lifted her gaze and our eyes fused, the entire world stopping on its axis as her green eyes met mine. Another moment burned into my soul, and I knew that somehow, she'd impact my life in ways I could only begin to grasp.

The entire room fell into chaos as the authorities descended on me. They couldn't let my insolence go unpunished, not while the entire town watched. I felt solid hands on my arms. I allowed them to restrain me, going limp as they clamped shackles on my wrists. Anxiety flared in my chest as I lost sight of her, the girl that was turning my well-laid plans on their head. But I'd achieved what I set out to accomplish.

# CHAPTER FIVE
## -WITCH-

### James

I was remanded to the provost marshal at the watch house, the only place in town to hold vagrants awaiting trial or punishment.

"You like witches?" The marshal chuckled in my ear as he led me toward the darkened hallway of awaiting cages. The sun was sinking low, the glow of candlelight adding to the suffocating heat of late summer. "Looks like it's your lucky day." The shackles fell from my hands the moment before I felt a boot on my back. The marshal pushed me forward, and

I stumbled into the waiting cell. The click of metal solidified my imprisonment as the heavy steel door locked behind me.

As my eyes adjusted to the dim light, my gaze swept the adjoining cells. A sigh escaped my lips when my eyes settled on the mop of blonde hair in the cell next to mine. *Thank the Divine!* My plan had worked and an entire night with my mystery witch stretched out before me.

She sat crouched in the corner, her eyes fixated on the ground, no hint of emotion on her face.

"Is it true what they say? Are you really a witch?" I asked, resting my forearms against the bars that separated us. Her eyes darted in my direction, glaring daggers at me.

"You!" she accused, doing nothing to hide the contempt in her voice.

"The name's James," I said smugly. "Nice to meet you, Katherine. Now, you were about to enlighten me with your knowledge of the dark arts."

"Go to hell," she sneered, turning her emerald gaze away from me.

"Looks like you're already on your way there. Maybe now is a good time to confess your sins."

She stared off into oblivion, her full lips pressed together in a thin line. Fully prepared to ignore me. But little did she know that I could be quite convincing.

"I hear you're an orphan. Did they find you on a faerie hill?"

"So I'm a changeling now? You people are so naïve," she

huffed. I couldn't hide the smirk that crept across my face. I'd managed to get a response from her.

"Naïve? Everyone knows that fae walk among us. Maybe 'witch' isn't an appropriate term for someone like you."

"Someone like me? You mean an educated woman with a mind of her own? I guess society isn't ready for a woman like that."

"Do all educated women kill their lovers?" I knew I was pushing my luck, but I couldn't help it. She was beguiling, and her fiery responses only fanned my curiosity.

"He was *not* my lover," she said poignantly.

"That part was my own embellishment. It's the part where you killed him that has me intrigued."

"You're awfully well versed for the town drunk. Maybe *you* aren't who you're perceived to be, either." I ignored her astute observations, keeping the focus on her. "I've always wondered how a witch commits murder."

"A simple understanding of plants is all you need to create the most deadly of concoctions. Nature is a much more effective killer than witchcraft could ever be."

"Ahh, so poison is your weapon of choice? Very poetic, but not nearly as much fun if you had been a witch." I felt my hopes of finding a fae in this beautiful woman slip through my fingers. "Why did you do it?" My words were sincere this time. I was vested in her story now and I had to know more.

"If you prick us, do we not bleed? If you tickle us, do we not laugh? If you poison us, do we not die? And if you wrong us, shall we not revenge?" Her prose was perfect as she quoted The Merchant of Venice. Her words collided into me, leaving me awestruck. I felt the demon in my chest stir, recognizing a kindred spirit.

I shook my head, dispersing the cascade of feelings running amuck in my mind.

"Shakespeare?" I grumbled, clearing my throat.

"The Bible isn't the only suitable reading material for a woman," she retorted.

"I take it you were due for your pound of flesh then?" I asked, but she turned away from me as though she intended to end our conversation. She was a vision in the candlelight. The flames highlighting her high cheekbones and straight nose. Her hair was illuminated, a glowing halo surrounding her. I knew I had to do something. If she was truly a witch, she was weaving a captivating spell over my heart, and I was desperate to find a way to save her.

"And here I was, thinking I had the privilege of encountering a real witch. But in reality, you're nothing more than a simple, jaded woman," I said dismissively. Pushing her buttons seemed to be the only way to get her to engage.

This obviously hit a nerve, because she turned her narrowed gaze at me and rose to her feet.

"I am a lot of things, Mr. James. But one thing I assuredly am not is a simple woman." She closed the space between us, and my mouth went dry as she approached. "There are no 'simple' women. We all have our tragedy to tell. Mine is of a girl with a secret gift, one that was hidden away, protected—

cherished. Until your God had other plans for her. Now, I am an abomination, a freak, a demon, and any number of horrible things. Anything but a young woman alone in an evil world."

She reached out, softly running her fingertips over the back of my hand. I froze. The feel of her soft touch sent shivers over my entire body. Her fingertips settled on my wrist at my pulse point. I could feel my heartbeat pounding away under her touch and then her eyes rolled back in her head. I stared, entranced in the moment. I should have been concerned for her health. I should have called for help. But I was the one who felt vulnerable. I couldn't pinpoint what was happening, but I knew my soul was laid bare for her. She was being shown things that only the Divine could know.

The moment her eyes popped open, she tore her hand away from me. A flicker of curiosity was quickly replaced by fear.

"Who *are* you?" she breathed, her chest heaving as she backed away from me.

"You have the sight," I whispered. It was only a guess, but I could see the truth of it flicker in her eyes. "What did you see?"

Our conversation was interrupted by the sound of heavy boots entering the cell block. In the next instant, Teach's imposing figure blotted out the candlelight. He was shrouded in darkness, but I could almost imagine the scowl on his face.

"Captain... I, umm... I..." My words trailed off. I had no

excuse to offer, and I knew lying to him now would only make my situation worse.

"I'm waiting, James," he said. The calm authority in his voice made me cringe.

"Waiting for you to give me something, anything resembling a reasonable excuse for defying my orders." His voice rose as he continued.

"I didn't defy you, Captain."

I jumped when his fists collided with the iron bars, the entire cage shaking with the force of it. "You would dare lie to me! And to my face, no less! I bring you on, raise you to a place of privilege among my men and not two days past you've already fucked up. Tell me, was I wrong, James? Did I make an error when I chose you as my bo'sun?"

"No, Captain. My sincere apologies. I finished my work, did your bidding. I only looked into the girl on my own time." I held my hands up, placating him as best I could. My only chance at escaping his wrath was to offer him something of value. "And it wasn't in vain. The girl… she can be useful to us."

Teach's full bellied laugh reverberated off the cages. "I have no need of a girl, even one so pretty. They are a dime a dozen, my boy. You'll figure that out in time. Never, ever let a pretty face sway your heart. Now get your drunk ass out of that cell." He produced a key, unlocking my cell and pushing the rusted door open. "I've pulled in some favors to get you out. And you will pay me back for them, with interest," he said as he turned to leave.

"But, Captain, listen to me. She has the sight. We could use her. I know you've been searching for something. I don't know what it is yet, but maybe she can help." I felt desperate, pleading my case to a hard man who wasn't easily swayed. He stopped then, appraising me with new eyes.

"You're more perceptive than I gave you credit for," he mused as he stroked his black beard. I took his moment of contemplation and pushed.

"She had a vision when she touched me just now."

"Is that true, witch?" he barked at her, shifting his intimidating gaze to Katherine, who was crouched at the back corner of her cell.

"I'm not a witch," she argued, and I winced. Her flippant mouth wouldn't get her very far with Teach. The damn woman had no concern when it came to her own self-preservation. "But he tells the truth. I've had visions."

"If that's so, then tell me something I don't already know, and just maybe you'll save yourself from a fiery demise," Teach challenged.

Katherine approached the iron bar separating her from Teach's imposing figure. I couldn't see her face, but her hesitation was well warranted. Teach was equally as lethal as the pyre that already had her name on it. She was bartering with the devil. Possibly selling her soul for an alternative darkness. Sometimes it was easier to accept a path of obscurity than welcome the evil you knew was coming for you.

She placed her hands tentatively on Teaches, connecting

with his pulse point until her head dropped back. Teach's eyes flashed with excitement, a grin pulling at his lips. When her eyes popped open, Teach shifted, catching her wrist in his iron grip.

"Tell me, sweetness, what did you see?" She peered over at me, her green eyes thoughtful for a moment before she leaned into him, whispering her secrets. Irritation bubbled up from my gut. She'd seen things about me, too. Yet she kept that to herself. Maybe she had seen her salvation in Edward Teach's future, but damned if I could curb the irrational pang of jealousy taking root in my chest.

"Time to go, James," he said as he broke away from her, a satisfied look on his face.

"And what about the girl?"

"What about her? You have the balls to question me after the shit you pulled tonight? You're lucky that I came baring a set of keys rather than a pistol."

I'D PACED my room all night long, flipping the tiny vial of faerie dust in my hand. The one thing I kept over Teach's head. My most valued possession. I'd been brought back to *Queen Anne's Revenge* with explicit instructions to remain in my quarters. I was on the verge of madness. My thoughts wouldn't give me a moment's peace. Katherine infected me like a plague, eating away at my soul until all I could see in my mind's eye was her.

I had no idea if her words had swayed Teach, and I made a desperate plea to the Divine to spare her life. I hadn't slept all night, time slowly leaching away as it marched toward her death sentence. I'd decided that I would remain in my room until dawn, but if Teach didn't call for me, I was going after her. With or without his help. When the latch creaked just before dawn, my pacing ceased as Teach entered the small space.

"If we're going to do this, then I'll need you at my side. The men won't like it, but that cannot be helped. She's a rare gem, and I must possess the power she yields."

I nodded my approval, but remained silent. I wouldn't rile the man with the heated words that lingered on my tongue. I shouldered past him as I headed for the main deck, but he grabbed ahold of my shoulder in his firm grip.

"I cannot condone your actions tonight, and you *will* pay for them, but I would be remiss if I didn't commend you on finding such a diamond in the rough. I knew I chose correctly when I selected you as bo'sun."

Teach never explained his plan to me, but I followed him without a word. He had connections in South Carolina, ones that turned a blind eye to our piracy and benefited handsomely from their connection to Teach. That continued to bring him back to the colony, and I was counting on those connections to pull this off.

He led me to an upscale section of town. Large brick

homes painted in bright colors lined the cobbled street. The dark skies had shifted, indicating the dawn was imminent, but our presence was still cloaked in darkness. We came to a large white home at the end of the street. Teach took the small alleyway to the back of the house, letting himself into the courtyard and wrapping his knuckles on the back door.

"Edward!" A voice hissed when the door creaked open. "What in the Devil—"

"Fuck your Devil, Raskin. I believe you'll find me to be a trifle worse. Now let me in." Teach shouldered past the bewildered old man, and I followed behind.

"You better have a good reason to show yourself at my house. Someone could have seen you," the man grumbled as he led us down a darkened hallway. His small oil lamp casting us in deep shadows against the walls. We entered a neatly appointed study. The walls lined with bookshelves; a mahogany desk set at the far end of the room. As the old man went around lighting several candelabras, Teach motioned me to have a seat in one of the leather upholstered chairs. The room dripped with wealth and my mind began to question just who this man might be.

When he finally settled himself behind the desk, recognition hit me. He was dressed in a linen nightshirt, but this was the judge who'd proceeded over Katherine's case. I remembered his wrinkled scowl; the same one he wore now. His powdered wig was replaced by a rumpled nightcap, but I knew I wasn't mistaken.

"You have my attention, Edward. What's so important that it couldn't wait till morning?"

"I need someone released from the watch house," he stated bluntly as he pulled a rolled cigarette from his belt. He struck a match on the fine desk and lit it, the end flaring red.

"Have you gone daft? You barge into my home, risking my reputation, all for what? Because you can't keep a handle on your crew!" I flinched when Teach's fist slammed on the desk, its entire contents rattling with the force of the blow.

"Don't you ever lecture me on how I run my crew!" Teach's voice bellowed in the small room and the decrepit old man only stared in shock, his Adam's apple bobbing as he swallowed. "Now, there is a girl being held at the watch house. I need you to release her to me."

"A girl?"

"Yes, a girl. A witch, as you'd like to call her."

"Surely you can't mean—"

"Katherine is her name, and yes, that is exactly who he means," I snarled, unable to keep my mouth shut. The old man peered at me briefly before dismissing me altogether, returning his gaze to Teach.

"Surely there are other whores in town that will fulfill your needs. This case is of particular interest to the governor. I can't—" Teach was a flash of movement at my side. In the blink of an eye, he'd reached across the desk, lifting the man from his chair by his neck.

"I grow tired of your insolence! Have you forgotten that I

own you?" Teach reached for the man's sleeve, tearing it open to reveal a scar of a skull and crossbones on his forearm. Teach placed his finger on the scar. The man began to writhe and squeal in Teach's tight grip. Smoke curled up from his arm and the scent of burning flesh filled the air. "You will release the girl into my custody. I don't care what story you have to tell, what poor soul you'll have to pin it on, just make sure it's done. If you fuck with me, I will shut down the entire harbor and lay siege to your city until it crumbles under my boot." Teach dropped the man just as quickly as he had grabbed him, and he collapsed in his chair, cradling the offended arm to his chest.

"The governor... he, he won't be pleased. He'll know it was me! He'll have my head for it," the man sobbed.

"Tell Nathaniel that I'm calling in my favor. Trust me, he'll know exactly what you mean, and won't give you any more trouble."

"Yes, Captain. I will have her delivered to you at *Queen Anne's Revenge*. I shall go to the watch house and oversee it personally."

"Oh, and Raskin, do keep your hands to yourself. I don't want your filth contaminating my property."

# CHAPTER SIX
## -SUPERSTITION-

### James

The early morning sun shimmered off Katherine's blonde waves as we made our way aboard *Queen Anne's Revenge*. Even in its mussed state, her hair seemed to glisten like spun gold. She was a divine gift wrapped in tattered rags, shining through the dirt and grime of society's misgivings.

"James, I'm assigning Miss Hawkins' care to you, and you alone. No one is to touch her without my permission. Lest they lose their goddamn hands!" Teach barked the orders loudly for the entire crew to hear. We had left port for

Nassau the moment we'd returned. Collecting Katherine had been more of a challenge than we bargained for, and the delay had thrown us completely off schedule. Teach wasn't overly thrilled about it either; and his mood reflected the inconvenience.

"But, Captain," someone grumbled from the back of the ship. "She'll bring ill luck to the *Queen Anne*. We can't have a woman aboard." The crew started to whisper doubt amongst themselves as a nervous energy spread like wildfire across the main deck.

Katherine's eyes went wide at the remark, and she clutched at a necklace she wore, obviously drawing some comfort from the simple piece of jewelry. She hadn't uttered a single word since boarding the ship. The realities of being trapped at sea with a bunch of lawless pirates was quickly becoming clear. I hadn't given much thought to whether or not the crew would accept her presence on board. I'd been more concerned with what she could offer me in my search for faerie dust.

"Who said that?" Teach demanded. "Step forward now and reveal yourself."

"It was I, Captain." Auggie, a scruffy older fellow, stepped forward, his head held high. Clearly confident in his convictions. "She will anger the sea gods, sir. She must go." The crew grumbled in agreement.

"Well then..." Teach pandered. "I guess we'll need to offer a sacrifice." He paused for a moment, stroking his beard.

Auggie's face scrunched in confusion. "Bare her breasts!"

someone shouted from behind. "It's the only way to calm Manann."

I pulled Katherine closer to my side. No one was going to touch her. I was the reason she was here, and the burden of her safety fell on me.

A sinister smile slid across Teach's face. "Toss him overboard," he said it nonchalantly, as though Auggie's life meant nothing.

The crew stood silent, frozen in shock. No one moved or dare speak a word. It was a well known nautical superstition that women aboard ships brought bad luck. But the crew had also sworn an oath to abide pirate code. One didn't question your captain's orders. Especially one like Teach. He was known for his brutality and governing his ship with an iron fist.

I looked over at Katherine and wondered if she would ultimately be the demise of *Queen Anne's Revenge*. It was hard to believe that a seemingly demure, broken woman could single-handedly take down a massive vessel like the *Queen Anne*. It would be worth it. I'd sink a hundred ships with her if it meant I could get back to Neverland and get my revenge on Pan. That bastard had eluded me long enough. I was drowning in the murky depths of abhorrence. Reveling in the sweet suffocation.

"James!" Teach's shrill voice pulled me from my reverie. "Don't just stand there. Toss him." The crew remained silent, staring at me. I tried desperately to find the strength to follow the captain's orders. I had no choice. It was kill or be killed. Auggie's fate was sealed whether I obliged or not.

"Mr. James," Auggie stared at me wide eyed as I approached. "Please, sir. I have a family to feed. Please," he begged, breaking my heart.

"Now!" Teach demanded.

I grabbed Auggie, blocking out his incessant pleading, and tossed his fragile form, along with a piece of my humanity, off the edge of the ship with a resounding splash.

"Let that serve as a reminder," Teach barked. "You pledged a vow of fealty. No one questions my orders. Miss Hawkins is my personal property. If anyone has a problem with her being aboard, you are free to jump ship and try your luck with Manann. Get back to work! James."

"Aye, Captain."

"Get Miss Hawkins cleaned up and settled in her room. I'm suddenly feeling the need to release some tension."

I ESCORTED Katherine below deck to a cabin just outside of Teach's. It was a confined space. Nothing but a small bed and a desk. A single candle offered comfort and light in the shadows. It wasn't much, but it was her own. I feared it would soon become her safe haven. "This will be your room, Miss Hawkins."

"I guess it's better than a cell," she mumbled while looking out the porthole. "At least I can see daylight."

"I'll be keeping the door locked for now." I informed her, awaiting some fiery response.

"Locked? Am I to be a prisoner?"

"Having you aboard will be a temptation for some and a bad omen for others. Either way, keeping you barred inside will insure your safety." At least having her under lock and key would protect her from the crew, but Teach was another story. I had seen him with the whores at *The Gilded Filly*. He had unusual tastes when it came to carnal activities, and I feared he would soon break our little witch.

"So the answer is yes."

I sighed. "Would you rather I leave you at the mercy of these men? To be raped, beaten, or worse?"

"You think I can't protect myself? I'm a strong woman, Mr. James," she boasted. "What about your Captain? Can you protect me from him, too?"

I had the decency to look down at my hands as she called me out on my failed attempt at chivalry. Here I was, explaining how I'd protect her from the crew, all the while knowing I wouldn't lift a finger to save her from Teach.

"I'm sure you are capable, Miss Hawkins. But the door stays locked."

Truth was, I didn't trust her not to sacrifice herself to the sea once Teach was through with her. I wouldn't risk losing her until I got answers. Plus, the idea of one of Teach's men getting their filthy hands on her had me feeling unusually protective. I didn't like the thought of Teach touching her, either. But that was a fate I'd have to accept.

She stood silently, taking in the small space as I removed the shackles from her bruised wrists. "While you are in this room, you will be free to move about." I turned her wrists, inspecting the damage. They were more than bruised. Her skin was raw and oozing. If I ever met a man who could do such vile things to a helpless woman, I'd delight in removing his hands. My fingers lingered a bit too long on her soft, delicate skin, drawing her attention back to me. Our eyes locked, and for a moment, time stopped. My heart pounded in my chest. This woman stirred something deep with in me. A curiosity for the future. A desire that I feared had the power to consume my soul. And it was clear in that moment that she felt something, too.

A loud knock on her cabin door startled us both back into action. Crew members barged in carrying Teach's private tub. One by one, they brought in buckets of hot water from the galley, filling a steaming bath for our guest.

"Warm water," I mused. "You must have made an impression. The Captain doesn't do simple pleasures. No one gets a warm bath. Not even Teach himself."

"Simple pleasures," Katherine huffed under her breath. "I'm sure he'll be finding his pleasures in my company."

She was right. Teach was clearly not just interested in her abilities to see the future. I was no stranger to the debauchery at which she would be expected to endure. She didn't deserve what he would surely do to her.

"I'll give you some privacy." I turned to look back at her before leaving. She was filthy, her clothing was worn and tattered. She had been through hell already and, unfortunately, this ship would not be her redemption. I would do what I could to raise her from perdition, but my powers were limited. "I'll return shortly with bandages for your wrists and some fresh clothing. If you need anything, please ask."

"Could you bother the cook for some honey?" she asked demurely. "For my wounds."

"Honey? For your wounds? Are you sure you're not a witch?" I chuckled. Cook was going to think I'd gone insane. "I'll try, but I make no promises."

"I'm not a witch," she grumbled under her breath, holding strong in her convictions. I turned to look at her one last time before locking her safely in her room. I couldn't decipher if she was happy to have avoided a fiery death, or contemplating throwing herself overboard. Her life here on Queen Anne's Revenge would not be an easy one. And I feared Teach would destroy her before I got what I so desperately wanted.


KATHERINE WAS STILL SOAKING in the bath when I returned. Her blonde hair was piled high atop her head. Damp tendrils framed her beautiful face. Her cheeks were flushed from the warm water, lending a seductive glow to her already ethereal features. Before I could utter a word, Katherine stood, leaving me speechless. Water glistened as it ran over her voluptuous curves and my jaw dropped. Despite her bruised frame, her body was perfection. A beautifully sculpted masterpiece, and she made no effort to conceal it. She had the most exquisite breasts I had ever seen; full and perky. Pink nipples, the perfect shade of blushed rose, were taut with chill. Her waist was tiny, yet soft and drew my eyes down to her ample hips and thighs. I could feel my cock growing hard. I'd never seen such beauty. I shut my eyes and quickly turned around. Temptation be damned. I could not have her. Teach would destroy me just for thinking about it.

"Milady, I... I... I've brought you some clothes." My words stammered as I redirected my thoughts, and thrust the dress behind me.

"Does my nakedness offend you, Mr. James?" Her voice was riddled with seduction.

I chuckled under my breath. "I've seen my fair share of naked women. I'm simply offering you privacy. Something you'll soon learn, my captain won't afford you."

"Women's clothes? I was expecting breeches and a tunic. Does your captain make a habit of collecting women for his pleasures?"

"Teach keeps a 'collection' if you will of women's clothing. I'm not sure exactly what he does with them. Sometimes he gifts them to his whores."

"Whores?" she questioned. "If he has whores, then why does he need me?"

"Because you, milady, are an exquisite beauty and your abilities allow him the excuse of keeping you within reach."

"You may turn around now," she sighed. "If I'm to wear this ridiculous gown, I'll need your help tying my stays."

She had slipped on her shift. The dampness of her skin added a transparency to the now clinging fabric. Her pink pert nipples were on display, and I could not advert my eyes. The memory of her naked body would forever ravage my mind. She slid on her stays and turned her back to me.

"I've had plenty of practice undressing women, but I've never helped one dress," I confessed as I grabbed ahold of the laces and gave a tug.

"Not too tight!" she pleaded. "I've never been a fan of all this... costumery." She huffed, tugging on the corset, clearly unhappy with the offered dress. "How is one supposed to breathe?"

"I'm sorry you find the clothing unsatisfactory. It is what the captain prefers."

Katherine turned around, a vision of beauty in a black brocade silk mantua. The dress pushed her large breasts up into a delicious swell that threatened to spill over with each breath. The corsetry accented her generous curves giving her that undeniable hourglass figure. She was pure perfection. A petite porcelain doll for Teach to play with. Jealousy stirred in my heart. She was forbidden fruit, and I longed for a taste. Katherine's words resonated with me. How was I supposed to breathe when this woman took my breath away?

# CHAPTER SEVEN
## -ALCHEMY-
### Katherine

"Wake up!"

The sound of Edward's voice outside my door roused me mere moments before I heard a loud thud.

"Ugh!" James gasped, "Captain, I... I—"

"What are you doing outside of Katherine's door, James?" Edward chided. "Get up! Before my boot finds your ribs again."

I laid still, frozen on the floor in fear, silently listening as James let out a painful groan.

Late last night, hours after he'd locked me into my

makeshift prison, I'd heard James clearing his throat. He had been sitting outside my door. He claimed to be keeping watch, that he didn't trust the crew members. But I got the feeling it was more than that. We sat with the door between us in silence, our fingers entwined for what felt like hours. I found a simple comfort in his presence. Reassurance in the warm caress of his thumb. I felt safe. Enough so that I was able to fall asleep soundly for the first time in what felt like weeks.

"I was just protecting your property, Captain. I heard rumors that the crew was planning a late night break in."

"My crew knows better than to cross me. This girl will be the death of you. What did I tell you about a pretty face? Get your ass back on deck where you belong. And James."

"Aye?"

"Don't let Miss Hawkins keep you from your duties, bo'sun, or I'll have that title stripped from your position."

"Aye, Captain."

I waited a moment for Edward to walk away before sliding my fingers under the door. A silent acknowledgment of my appreciation. A desperate plea for reassurance. Did we share something special last night, or was I just longing for companionship? His fingers found mine, linking us together briefly. My heart fluttered at the feel of his touch, and just as quickly as it began, he let go and made his way down the hall. Leaving me alone with my thoughts, yet again.

. . .

JAMES MADE a nightly habit of visiting through my door. Sometimes it was brief, sometimes we sat for hours silently, our fingers entwined. We had been spending a great deal of time together and I indulged our growing friendship. Long days at sea seemed less daunting while in his presence. He was the only person on this ship with whom I found an ounce of kindness. He seemed to actually care about my wellbeing and not just my ability to satisfy a need. Although he looked at me like he wanted to devour me, he had never touched me inappropriately. James was a handsome man. Tall and fit. Blonde wavy hair, kissed by the sun. Piercing forget-me-not blue eyes, rimmed in kohl. A strong jaw line. I wondered what his body looked like. What his kisses felt like. Was his beard soft, or rough like Edward's? Was he a gentle lover or a sexual deviant? I found myself wishing I was *his* property.

Edward had made me his plaything. His interests were dark in nature. He was not your typical man. He enjoyed inflicting pain. I think he got off on it. The more I cried out, the harder he went. If I were being honest with myself, I did find some pleasure in the pain. It gave me reason to feel the way I did, to justify my tears. I had no choice in the matter. I was his property. I could either play along, or fight at every corner. It was simply easier to just accept my fate.

*CRACK!*

I gasped, surprised by the immense intensity of the pain. The sound of the whip only seemed to deepen the burn. Like a million bees stinging my back, my skin was set ablaze.

*Crack!*

I cried out this time, unable to hold back the tears. I could feel a warm trickle of blood spilling down my backside and down my thighs. My vision began to blur. My endorphins rushed to anesthetize my broken spirit.

*Crack!*

The world around me was caving in. The pain was too much. Darkness descended upon me as my legs gave out.

"I'm not done with you yet." He slapped my ass, rousing me from my stupor. "Wake up!" His words were harsh and demanding. I could feel Edward releasing me from the shackles. The only thing keeping me standing. He draped my limp body over the edge of the bed. Spreading my weak legs with his knee, exposing my core, and allowing him access. He smeared the blood from my wounds across my ass and between my sex, mixing it with my arousal.

A shameful moan escaped my throat as he pushed into my wetness. I couldn't hide my pleasure from Edward. My body betrayed me, and he sought out the sick part of me that enjoyed his torture. I hated this part of me. The broken, deviant side.

"Your pussy is dripping for me. You like the pain, don't you?" His voice was laden with lust.

I tried to muffle my pleasure as he thrust deeper and

deeper, pounding away at my broken body. Hoping this would be the time I'd get my release—that the pain would somehow end in pleasure. Just as quickly as he began to thrust, he grunted, jerking his hips as he climaxed, leaving me broken, bleeding, and wanting. Unsatisfied yet again. I was simply for his pleasure. I didn't deserve release.

"Well done, my pet," Edward praised as he pulled his cock from my battered body. "I'll send in James to clean you up," I laid motionless on the edge of the dirty mattress. Edward had never whipped me before. The pain had pushed me to my limit. If I was going to survive Edward's torment, I was going to need help. It was time to wield my magic.

"Katherine," James gasped as he entered the room. I hated that he had to see me like this. "What has he done this time?" He leaned down, wrapping me in the bloodied sheets and scooped me up into his arms.

"Whip," I murmured. The weight of my body pressing against my wounds brought me painfully back to reality. "Gentle," I pleaded, as tears streamed down my cheeks and shame filled my heart.

"I'm so sorry. We're going back to your room now. You are safe with me." He tried to reassure me, and I wanted to believe him. It was not lost on me that he was the reason I was here in Edward's possession.

"In my desk," I whimpered. "There is a list. A list of things I need. Take it to the cook and bring it back. Quickly," I pleaded. I had made the list my first night aboard *Queen*

*Anne's Revenge.* I had no idea what to expect from Edward, and until now I had managed without it.

He set me down on the bed gently. Peeling back the sheet and assessing my wounds. His hands hovered over my broken skin. "You're going to need bandages."

"Bring an empty rum bottle with you. James, don't leave me alone long."

Concern was plastered on his typically stoic face. He turned to look at me before leaving the room. "You have my word. I'll be right back."

"WHAT IS ALL OF THIS FOR?" James asked as he placed the collection of herbs on the desk. Along with a pitcher of fresh water and a bowl of rags.

"It's for pain," I winced trying to stand up. "Help me to the desk. Please."

"Let me clean your wounds first."

"No!" I barked, holding out my arms to stop him. "I'm sorry. Let me do this first. You can clean my wounds after." I reached for the bowl and dumped out the rags. I needed relief fast. I didn't care if James saw me working magic. It was a risk I had to take. I had no choice. If he exposed me, I would accept my fate. Death would be an easier path than what Edward seemed to have in mind for me. I placed the herbs in the bowl and topped them with fresh water. Closing my eyes and holding my hands over the bowl, I shifted my focus, calling on the embodiment of Earth itself, Gaia.

"*Serenus potentia, doloris levis esse, virtus herbis, transmutare ex aromata. Pax et conforto, dolor recede, hoc elixir fiat, auxilium concede.*"

I poured the elixir into the empty rum bottle and took a small sip, sighing with relief as all my pain instantly vanished. I wrapped myself tightly in my sheet, covering my nakedness and shielding my newly exposed truth.

The elixir was colorless and odorless. I would be able to pass it off as mere water. Edward would be none the wiser and I could continue my service pain-free. I said a silent thank you to Gaia and turned to see James wide eyed, his mouth gaped open in disbelief.

"What did I just witness?"

"I'm not a witch." I spoke the words with conviction, hoping he would let it go.

"Then what are you, Katherine? What was that? What did you just drink?"

"It's a simple pain elixir. Nothing more."

"It certainly sounded like more."

"I am an alchemist."

"An alchemist or a witch? Are they not one and the same?"

"I don't like the word witch; it has an evil connotation to it. I'm not evil, James."

"I'm not implying that you are evil, Katherine. I'm just trying to understand who you are." He reached his hand out for mine, looking at me curiously, without the typical expression of damnation that I'd grown to expect. "The divine has bestowed gifts upon you, and that is a beautiful thing."

I felt my cheeks warm with his kind words. "I believe that nature is sacred. That there is power in the constant cycle of seasons. But beliefs such as that would have me burning at the stake. Especially if you adopt the title of witch. My parents were burned at the stake in front of my very eyes, all in the name of witchcraft," I admitted, feeling comfortable enough to lower my guard and share a bit of my past with him. "They weren't bad people. They were loving parents who knew how to wield the earth." I felt a tear roll down my cheek. It had been a long time since I'd allowed myself to think about them. "Society is filled with ignorance. People fear what they don't understand, and my parents paid the ultimate price." I could feel my walls snapping back into place. It was hard to let anyone, especially James, see my vulnerabilities, so I quickly wiped the evidence of them from my cheeks.

"How old were you? When they were burned?"

"Ten. That's the only reason I was spared. The church took me in and tried to 'correct' my upbringing. Only my parents had taught me the craft from a young age. For all they tried, the church couldn't purge my memories. I've practiced in secret ever since." I reached for my locket, rubbing the warm metal between my fingers. It was the only tangible piece of my parents I had left.

James sat quietly in thought for a moment. "Teach me."

"No, James," I shook my head, "I could never. It takes a lifetime to master."

"Do you want your secrets safe from Teach?"

I looked at him with disbelief. "Are you blackmailing me?" After all we had been through I thought James would have my back.

"Did it work?" He cocked his head to the side, raising his eyebrows and smirked.

I sighed. The last thing I needed was Edward knowing my true capabilities. James had me against a wall. "We would be bound by deceit. Edward could never find out. Surely he would have you run through for your transgressions. Never mind what he would do to me."

"It's a risk I'm willing to take. Besides, I'd rather be on the wrong side of Teach's blade than deny myself your exquisite company. It's not everyday you meet someone with your abilities. Allow me to be your humble student."

I pondered the idea for a moment. Having James bound to me through lies, though dangerous, could prove to be a bargaining tool. "I want a sketch pad and some pencils for my troubles."

He nodded. "I should be able to make that happen."

"You will have to dedicate your time to studying. If Edward finds out," I shook my head, "I will damn your mortal soul to a lifetime of excruciating pain, heartache, and misery. You will beg for his cutlass. Do you understand?"

"Yes, Magister," he mocked. "We can start tomorrow. Now let me clean those wounds." He turned me around tugging on the sheet to expose my back. "The lacerations haven't begun to heal," he stated surprised to find them just as gruesome as before.

"The elixir only takes the pain away. Magic has boundaries. They will have to heal on their own."

"Now that we are bound by secrets. You can tell me what you saw that day, back in the watch house," he began to dab at my ragged skin, "When you saw my future."

I sighed, knowing he wouldn't be satisfied with my answer. "I saw a shining, silver hook. Nothing more, nothing less." I wasn't certain what the visions had been trying to unveil, it was shrouded in darkness. There was more to him than he let on. He was definitely hiding something. Things the universe wanted to keep hidden, even from me. One thing was certain, his path wouldn't be an easy one.

"You saw a hook?" He paused cleaning my wounds, "What exactly does that mean?" he pleaded.

I shrugged my shoulders. "Sometimes the visions aren't clear."

"We will try again." His words were an order.

"Oh? Are you going to treat me like Edward now? First you blackmail me, and now this. Am I supposed to be at your beck and call?"

He slammed his fist on my desk frustrated, startling me. "I can be like Teach if that's what you prefer. Try again," he demanded. His normally calm composure replaced with hostility.

I turned around interrupting his incessant dabbing and

glared at him, angry with his attempt to intimidate me. I reached out and grabbed his wrist. Sliding my fingers over his warm skin, settling over his pulsing veins. His heart was racing, he was nervous. Instantly, I felt the link between us begin to course through my body. My eyes rolled back as visions flashed across my mind's eye.

Blood red tainted everything.

A pattern of stars in the night sky.

Revenge, rage, deceit.

Family—an auburn haired lost boy.

Petrichor filled my nostrils, I heard crowing off in the distance.

A strange, yet beautiful land.

A shining hook.

Aubergine dripping from a heart wrapped in roots.

Obsession.

The sweet smell of hydrangea mixed with campanula.

A crimson stain seeping up through ivory satin.

Agony, defeat.

I ripped my hand from his wrist and tried to hide my shock. James was not exactly who he pretended to be. I just wasn't sure exactly what that meant, and my visions had only sparked more questions than answers. What *was* certain was that his future was cloaked in pain and anger.

"Well?" he prodded waiting for my response.

I composed myself. When the time was right, he'd spill his truth. And if he didn't, I'd eventually get deep enough to figure him out. Until then I decided to keep the details to myself. I had a feeling they would soon become valuable. I cocked my head to the side and smiled. "Blood red."

"Woman! You're killing me with suspense. Blood red what?" Was it the blood of my enemies?

"I don't know, James. I just saw the color."

He looked at me with contempt. "What about Teach? What did your visions tell you that day."

"He'll find what he's looking for. And so will his adversary."

"I've known for some time that Teach has been searching for something. He's had a hard-on for it since the day I met him. But an adversary? Teach is always watching his back. I had no idea there was a particular someone. Did you see what he is searching for?" James was like a dog with a bone.

"I'm not certain what it is, but I know its important to him and he won't stop searching until he finds it."

"What exactly is Teach hiding?" I wondered the same thing about James.

"I've heard him mumble the name Ruby in his sleep. Maybe she is who he is looking for? Or who he is hiding from?"

"Ruby," he pondered stroking his beard. "Like the *blood-red* gemstone?"

# CHAPTER EIGHT
## -CONFESSIONS-

### James

#### 1716

"Teach is up to something. I can smell it on him," Henry blurted out in the parlor of *The Gilded Filly*. We'd been drinking copious amounts of rum and it seemed to have loosened Henry's tongue. He was right, Teach had been off these last few weeks. Some were even saying that he had gone mad. He had taken to tucking lit cannon fuse in his beard as a method of intimidation. And it had proved to be quite effective. The crew were starting to think he was the devil incarnate.

"You'll be wise to lower your voice, my friend. Or find yourself walking the plank with Teach's cutlass at your back."

"The man's brain is addled," Henry whispered. The rum thick on his breath. "I heard him rambling on about the Tuatha Dé Danann just last night."

That caught my attention. The Tuatha Dé Danann were fae. Definitely not from Neverland, but fae none the less. This could be the lead I'd been patiently waiting for. But now was not the time to discuss the details. Teach was just a few walls away entertaining his favorite whore, Miss Charlotte. If memory served, he'd make quick work of her.

"All these years searching. In and out of random ports. Mysterious meetings. It's coming to a head. I can feel it, James."

"Enough about Teach. I fear your wagging tongue will turn you to fish food." I had to steer the conversation elsewhere. Henry was going to get us both executed. Besides, I had plans of my own for the evening and I was counting on the rum to give me the courage to follow through. I'd quietly pulled Madame Matisse aside upon our arrival and provided her with one of Kat's gowns. I asked that Miss Alice be wearing it privately, and offered double the fee for their silence and cooperation in the matter. "Which one of these fine fillies has your eye?"

"Sweet, blue eyed Mary," Henry marveled. "I hear she flows like a mighty river."

I chuckled at his response. "You enjoy a matronly woman?" I raised my brow, "Did your mum not let you suckle at her teat long enough?" I laughed. Mary had been with *The Gilded Filly* since my first days back across the Veil. She had aged well, but she was definitely one of the oldest women in the brothel.

"I've never been with a woman who overflows with pleasure." A smirk slid across his face. "I want to bathe in her sweet release." The rum definitely had Henry spilling his hidden desires. "Who is the lucky lady pulling your pole tonight?"

"Miss Alice has taken my interest."

"Alice? The new blonde girl with the big perky bubbies?"

I smiled in response before taking another swig of rum.

"She reminds you of Kat, doesn't she?" He sighed as the smile slid off his face. "That woman is going to be your demise, James."

I wasn't as sly as I had hoped. "It's true. The woman has bewitched me. Katherine is a love I can not afford. She is forbidden and yet no matter how many times I deny my feelings, they keep flooding back. It's just a matter of time before the dam comes tumbling down around me."

"Feelings? Have you gone mad like our dear captain?"

"Henry, I'm hopelessly lost in her spell. I don't know what to do. Maybe Miss Alice can help release the ever-growing pressure."

"For your sake, and hers, I hope it works. Katherine is off limits, my friend, and Teach won't be merciful if he finds out you have developed feelings for his prized possession. Does she know?"

"No, she doesn't, and I'd like to keep it that way." I hadn't made my feelings known to Kat. Our relationship was already flirting with danger. I'd taken every opportunity I could to sneak off to her room. At first, I'd used our little agreement as a means to rationalize the visits. We'd spent countless hours together while she taught me the art of alchemy, but I'd long since conceded that it was her company that kept me eager to return and not the tutoring. Taking things further would only prove deadly. "Why don't you find Miss Mary before you come to your senses. Go… swim in her salty seas, my friend." I shooed him off before he could continue his questioning.

Teach's obsession with Katherine had only grown with time, and I prayed to the Divine he would tire of her soon. It was becoming increasingly harder to watch him use her over and over for his carnal desires. He had never questioned the amount of time we'd been spending together. He trusted me. I had pledged fealty and would never overstep my boundaries, and in many ways that was true. But I would not deny myself the light she brought to my once dull, dark days.

"EVERYTHING IS TO YOUR REQUEST, Mr. James," Madame Matisse assured. "You'll have our utmost discretion."

"Thank you, Madame." I bowed my head in respect and handed her a hefty sack of coin before entering the private space.

Miss Alice stood still in the center of the room, a vision

in emerald-green silk. The dim flickering of candlelight helped to blur the finer details of her face, allowing me, for the moment to believe that she was indeed my beloved Katherine. This was as close to touching her as I could get, and I was a desperate man. I needed to quench this thirst before I broke my fealty to Teach. I took a final hearty swig off the bottle of rum and made my way over to her.

"You can call me whatever pleases you," Alice cooed.

"Silence," I barked. "No speaking." I didn't want the sound of her voice to break the spell. If this was going to work, I needed to believe the mirage. I shook my spinning head and allowed myself to swim deeper into the illusion. "I've wanted this for so long." I brushed her blonde hair behind her shoulder before gripping her face and tilting her head to mine. I kissed her hard. My tongue exploring her hungry mouth, while my hands roamed freely over the silk gown, relishing in the curves of her body.

I turned her around and ripped the laces from the bodice, peeling it away from her skin. I reached my hands up, cupping her warm pillowed breasts and groaned at the feel of them in my hands. I pressed my cheek against her bare back, closing my eyes and embraced her petite form. The scent of Katherine still lingered on the fabric, spiraling me deeper into the fantasy. Her nipples peaked against my palms, begging to be touched. I pinched and pulled at them while biting the soft flesh of her shoulders, drawing out little mews of approval. My cock was hard as a rock. Years of suppressing my desire were about to come to a head. I needed release now.

I bent Alice over the bed, keeping her face away from mine and pulled her skirts up over her ass, exposing her slick slit. Reaching down between us, I dropped my breeches, pulling out my cock. I slid the tip through her wetness before sliding in ever so slowly, savoring the sensation of her sheathing me deep inside. Alice moaned as I buried myself to the hilt and started pumping into her. It had been far too long since I felt the warm, wet embrace of a woman. So much pent up temptation. I wouldn't last long.

"James?" I heard her voice before I noticed the light spilling in from the hall. I instantly froze. My heart broke into a million pieces. She was never meant to witness this. I quickly pulled out of Miss Alice and pulled up my breeches before turning to face my beloved.

"Kat? What are you doing here?" She was supposed to stay on the ship while we were at port. I prayed to the Divine that she would find a way to understand.

"It doesn't matter why. I'm here now. Is that my dress?" The look on her face was utter confusion. "James, why is this whore wearing my dress?"

"I—I uhh... I'll leave you two." Alice covered up her breasts and quickly left the room, shutting the door behind her.

"Katherine, please," I begged as tears formed in her eyes. "I needed. I couldn't—"

"I don't understand. What's happening?"

I walked closer as she backed up against the wall, trying to keep space between us as tears spilled down her cheeks.

"Please, Kat, don't cry. Please, forgive me, for I am a desperate man. Tell me that I disgust you," I pleaded. "I didn't mean to hurt you. Please, tell me you hate me. Release me from your spell."

"That is not an answer! You stole from me. One of the few possessions that I can call my own, and for what? To dress up your whore? Why? I need to know why, James." She stood with her hands fisted at her side, her cheeks streaked with angry tears. Her eyes searching for answers. Crushing my broken heart.

"There is no sense in trying to hide it anymore." I tried to rationalize my behavior. "I've fought to keep it to myself." I shook my head in an attempt to clear the buzz from the rum. "Katherine," I sighed. "I can't breathe without you. I... I love you."

"James." She shook her head no.

"You have bewitched me and stolen my heart. There is no other explanation. I'd rather die than deny myself your affections. I love you in ways that words can not convey."

"I love you too," she whispered the words, as if speaking them quietly would somehow negate the power of them.

"My sweet Katherine." I stepped closer closing the gap between us. I could feel her breathing becoming heavy. "I have waited years to hear you say those words. Say them again, so that I might lock them deep with in my soul, never to be forgotten." I pushed her hair away from her face and wiped the tears from her cheeks.

"I love you," she said with conviction, locking my heart in her grasp.

I pulled her face towards mine and sealed her lips with a righteous kiss. The world around me stopped spinning, and time stood still. Her mouth was the sweetest sin, and I was awash in her confession. She hesitated for only a moment before returning my affections. Pushing back into me with a fierce passion.

I nibbled at her ear, drawing out little sighs from her before bathing her neck in kisses. She smelled of frankincense, amber, and vanilla. Intoxicating my already heightened senses.

"But, I belong to another," she panted. Threatening to break the spell and sully the moment. I wouldn't have it. I finally had her to myself.

"Shhh, don't speak of him. Not now. In this moment—right here, right now—you are mine," I growled in her ear, claiming her. My hands began to roam over her silk-covered curves. "I've longed for you," I confessed. "I've fantasized about this moment for years. Of touching you like this." My fingers dipped below her bodice, finding her nipple.

"I've dreamt of your kisses," she whispered. "Your caress."

Her words sent me over the edge. I growled and ripped open the bodice of her dress, exposing her perfect breasts. "You are perfection embodied." I grabbed them both in my hands, gently squeezing.

Soft moans escaped her pretty mouth as I circled her pert nipple with my fingers before sucking it into my mouth. Flicking the peak with my tongue.

"Please," she begged between breaths, lifting her leg to my hip and grinding against my now throbbing cock. "I need you."

I slid my hands up her leg, hesitating at her garter for a brief moment before finding her core dripping with desire. She was ripe with need, and it pulled a growl of approval from my throat. "Mine."

She purred with pleasure as I swept my fingers through her wetness, gently circling her clit. "Tell me to stop, Katherine, because I won't be able to deny myself. I will break my vow right now and never look back."

"James," she cried out my name in pleasure. As I plunged a finger deep with in her core. "Stop." The word was clear. I wrestled with the desire to push her further and pulled away, putting space between us.

I slid my finger in to my mouth. Closing my eyes and savoring the sweet tang of her honey. She was forbidden fruit, and she tasted of ambrosia. I held her eyes in a predatory gaze. "You better run, my little kitty Kat. The dam has breached, and I won't be able to hold back."

"I'm sorry," she whispered as the tears threatened to spill again. "He'll kill us both."

"I won't give you up. Not now. Not when I know you love me." I stepped closer, closing the gap.

"Please, James, I can't." She pulled her tattered dress up over her breasts, struggling to cover herself.

I wouldn't force her. Not like he did. Fuck! This woman really was my demise. I ripped the dirty sheet off the bed, thrusting it towards her cowering frame. "Cloak yourself. Go straight back to the ship, Katherine. Stop for no one."

Her face paled with anxiety. "What if he finds me in the streets?"

"Let me handle Teach. Now, go before I lose all control and take you here and now."

She turned to look back at me one last time before running out the door.

My world had been turned upside down and all I managed to do was fuel the ever-growing pressure in my cock. I had to do something, or I was going to explode. I pulled my cock out of my breeches, closed my eyes, and began to stroke myself. I could still taste her on my tongue. Feel her slick folds on my fingers. Within a matter of moments, years of pent up tension were spilling down my shaft. I'd had a taste and now I wanted more. I wouldn't stop until she was mine.

I had to get back to the ship. Figure out what to do next. I left *The Gilded Filly* with a smile on my face and a spring in my step. For once, things were going in my favor.

# CHAPTER NINE
## -FAVORS-
### James

**M**y fingers dug into the splintered wood of the railing. Land was approaching. I could smell it rolling in off the mist and I counted down the moments until I could get off this ship. We'd been at sea for far too long. There was a time when I had found freedom on the open ocean. But over the last few months, the ship had become suffocating, a prison of my own making. Paranoia consumed me. It tainted every stolen moment I had with Kat.

I couldn't stay away from her. She was my drug of choice, and I was her helpless addict. It didn't matter that Teach would gut both of us if he ever found out. Now that I knew she felt the same, my desire for her had only intensified. It burned me from within, a charred ember in my chest. A constant reminder of her. But I needed some space. Some time to clear my head before my neurosis gave me away. We had made a vow to each other. We would wait until Katherine was no longer enslaved to Teach to be intimate. Sex would only make keeping our secret harder. Once she was mine, I wouldn't be able to look the other way. I wouldn't share her.

I felt his presence long before his hand landed solidly on my shoulder. My mind instantly began to race. Did he know? Was I already a dead man walking? Now I scrutinized even the simplest gestures from the man.

"Will you tell me now where we are headed, *Blackbeard*?" I asked, exaggerating the new moniker he'd earned for himself. Teach chuckled as he stroked his now infamous beard.

"Clew Bay."

"Ireland? You've taken us to fucking Ireland? What the hell for? You've sailed us all over the known world… and for what?" I didn't even try to hide my condemnation.

"You better watch your tone with me. I don't owe you any explanations. You follow orders! End of story," he barked, but then let out a deep sigh. I could tell the endless days at sea were getting to him as well. "I'm here to meet an old friend," he finally admitted. "I'm on the cusp, James. If things go as planned, we'll be off on a great adventure."

"Isn't that what we've been doing these last thirteen years?"

"Not like this. Nothing like what awaits us. Come, you must prepare yourself. We're heading inland to Castlebar. I'm leaving Drake behind with the crew to resupply the ship and make the repairs."

"Drake? But he's first mate. Those aren't his responsibilities, Captain."

"Let me worry about Drake. I need you with me this time."

The hairs on the back of my neck rose. An impromptu trip inland, just the captain and me—his lowly bo'sun. Would I ever return from this trip? My mind instantly went to Kat. If something happened to me, there would be no one to protect her.

"What about Kat?" The question came out before I could think better of asking it.

"Katherine? She'll remain in her room as usual. I'll get one of the crew—"

"Henry! I'll get Henry to take charge of her care in my absence," I blurted out. Even though I doubted any man on the ship would dare to touch the captain's property. I couldn't be too careful. After all, the threat to life and limb hadn't been enough to deter me. She'd been through more than any woman should have to bear. The guilt already ate away at me for not being able to save her from Teach.

"Fine, fine. Just be ready to leave the moment we drop anchor."

. . .

THE CREW BUZZED WITH EXCITEMENT, hurriedly preparing the ship to make berth. I took advantage of their distraction and slipped into Kat's room. She sat at her desk, her back turned to me. Sketching furiously on the pad of paper I'd given her. Charcoal covered the page in a depiction of a starry sky. She was lost in the moment, likely bringing one of her visions to life on the page. She was so peaceful. One of the few times when she didn't look like she had the world on her shoulders. I knew the news I was about to share would add to that burden. So I waited, memorizing her exactly as she was now, her golden hair in a cascade of chaos, falling around her charcoal smudged face. Her beauty put art to shame.

She paused, and I knew I'd broken the spell. Her emerald eyes turned to me, their light fading as she took me in. "James, is everything alright?" Concern lacing her voice. Apparently, I'd failed at masking my growing concerns. Once we were alone, I lingered with my back against the door. Taking a moment to let her nearness wash over me. Simply being in her presence was intoxicating. If this was the last time I laid my eyes on her, I wanted her image to be burned into my memory for eternity.

"We've made it to port," I answered. "He's taken us to Ireland. Teach is here to meet with someone, and he's insisting that I go with him."

The color drained from her face. "Do you think he knows?" she whispered.

"I can't say for sure. We've been careful, but…" I cleared my throat, unable to put words to that possibility. "I've arranged for Henry to take over my duties with you while I'm gone."

She nodded slowly. "Do you think he's meeting Ruby?" she deflected. I could see that her mind was racing with all the worst-case scenarios, but she was trying to hide it for my sake.

"Possibly. But I'm more concerned about you. If he knows, you aren't safe either. I want you to take this." I pulled a small blade from my belt. I reached for her hand and gently placed the dagger in her palm. The feel of her soft skin in my calloused hands made the fire flare in my chest. "Hide this under your pillow until I get back."

"And what if you don't come back? James, I can't lose you. I cannot do this without you," she pleaded with me.

"Then there is this." I pulled a small black vial from my belt. "If I don't come back, you'll have a choice. This will offer you a peaceful oblivion if you so desire it."

"Poison?" she guessed, her eyes going wide as she took in the bottle of black death in my hand. "How did you manage—"

"I've been practicing everything you taught me."

"You made this yourself?" she whispered, and I nodded solemnly. "I guess you're a better student than I gave you credit for." A half-hearted smile tugged at her lips. For a brief moment, fear was replaced by the look of pride in her eyes at my accomplishment and my heart swelled. What I would give to have her look at me like that everyday, but I wouldn't chance her suffering on the pleas of a man like me. My prayers to the Divine had always seemed to fall on deaf ears.

"I will leave you with a choice. This, "I emphasized, shaking the vial in her face, "is a better alternative than what he'll have planned for you."

I went to place the vial in her palm next to the blade, but she was trembling so violently that the dagger fell from her hand and landed in her thick skirts. I quickly collected the knife and tucked it safely under her pillow with the vial of poison. I knelt before her, taking her trembling hands in mine. Pressing my lips to her soft skin.

"Everything will be fine, Katherine. You don't have to worry. We'll figure something out soon and then we can be together. I'll take you away from all of this. Just give me a little more time, and we'll get out from under his thumb."

She nodded again, a silent tear leaking down her cheek.

"Do you trust me?"

Her emerald-green eyes raised to meet mine, and I was instantly entranced. Bewitched by her gaze alone.

"I trust you, James. Promise you'll come back to me?" She lifted her delicate hand from mine, her fine fingers running over my stubbled cheek.

"I swear it upon my unworthy heart. I will always come back for you." She leaned in, her mouth meeting mine in a frenzy. Her full lips were hard, needy, and urgent. I felt my body respond, running my fingers into her thick hair, pulling her closer. All our fears played out in that kiss.

"Take me now, James. We've waited so long. This could be our last chance to be together in this world. I want to feel your skin against mine. I want to know what it's like to have you inside of me. For once, I want to be filled with love," she panted, her soft words pleading with me to give her something that I couldn't. My body was on fire, desperate to claim her, make her mine. But I couldn't have her. Not like this. Not while she still belonged to Teach. Her words tore open my soul, and the need for her was almost too strong to control. I wanted to throw her on the bed and sink myself inside her, make her scream my name. But after we'd revealed our feelings that night at *The Gilded Filly*, we'd agreed to wait until we were free from Teach. Only when we could be together wholly and without the stain of Edward Teach, would we give ourselves to each other.

"No... no, I can't. You know we can't." I stumbled to my feet, needing to get some space before I caved completely and lost myself to my primal instincts.

"Why?"

"You know why. One day, Katherine, I will make you mine, but not like this. Not while he still owns a piece of you."

"You make it sound like that's something I can control," she shot back, looking wounded at my dismissal. A small tear slid down her cheek, and my resolve began to crack.

"I'm sorry. I know it's out of *both* our hands. I will make this right, Kat. Don't lose faith in me," I begged. How long would I be able to resist that which my heart so desperately desired? I knew I'd have to make a move soon.

"Before you leave, I want to give you something," she whispered, reaching under her pillow and pulling out the dagger I'd hidden there. With a quick flick of her wrist, she cut a small lock of her blonde hair.

"Take a piece of me with you." She handed the golden strands to me. I stared at the gift for a moment. It was risky. If Teach found it, it would be all the evidence he would need, but I couldn't say no. I didn't want to say no. I wrapped the silken hair around my finger and turned to go without saying goodbye. Goodbye was too final, and I refused to let this be the end for us.

I COULD FEEL his eyes boring into the back of my skull the entire trek to Castlebar. The rain and the swirling mist that shrouded the green isle didn't help to improve my mood. My shoulders were tense, my jaw clenched, and my hand gripped the pommel of my cutlass too tightly. The countless ways Teach could exact his revenge on me wreaked havoc on my nerves. But I'd be damned if I was going to go down easy. Pan and I had a date with destiny that I refused to miss, and I wouldn't let my feeble mortality get in the way.

"Who's so important that we have to travel five hours on

foot to Castlebar?" I asked. My fucking paranoia was relentless, but I was still curious. If I was wrong, and this had nothing to do with Kat and me, maybe I'd figure out more of Teach's mystery. At some point, Teach had turned from my mentor to my enemy. And one of the many things Teach had drilled into me over the years was, know your enemy better than yourself.

"I told you, an old friend."

I whirled on him; my temper easily roused. "You insisted you needed me on this trip. I think I deserve a little explanation. You've always told me, 'never go blind into any situation,' but now you expect me to look the other way for you. Open your eyes. I am not your obedient little dog anymore."

"Patience is a virtue," was all he said, no emotion on his face, no reaction to my volatile temper, which was uncharacteristic for the man I knew all too well.

"What do you know of virtue?" I spat at him.

"I know a great many things, James. I know you grow inpatient with me, but I told you long ago that only I can bring you what your soul truly desires. Your loyalty will not go unrewarded. I will explain everything at the proper time."

"Time is marching past with no hint of slowing, even for the likes of you. I cannot stand by and—"

"When it is time!" he bellowed, effectively silencing me. And I was left to ponder his veiled words for the rest of our journey.

We arrived at a neatly appointed pub by the time night

fell. Teach settled us at a small table in the back corner, perfectly situated to give us privacy and provide an ideal viewpoint of everyone in the pub. My clothes were soaked through, but the chill finally left me as the nearby fire warmed my bones. I fully expected Teach's friend to be waiting on us, but no one approached and Teach proceeded to order food and rum, settling in like we were simply weary travelers sharing a meal, rather than the notorious Blackbeard, here on business.

The man had garnered a name for himself across the known world. Becoming more myth than man. His behavior had become brazen over the years, bordering on psychotic. The tasks I'd carried out in his name would haunt me for the rest of my days. I'd seen more things I couldn't explain, and it only fanned the rumors. His reputation had grown even more than I think Teach had planned.

We sat in silence as my mind toiled over the choices I'd made in the last decade of my life. Thankfully, our glasses never sat empty. The ever attentive barmaid kept the rum flowing and for the first time in months, I allowed myself to drown out all of my troubles with drink, the knots of tension loosening with each glass. When my eyes grew heavy, and I thought I might pass out sitting at the table, the sound of chair legs dragging across the wooden floor brought me back to attention. A stranger sat down at the table across from Teach. Candlelight reflected off the stranger's vibrant green cloak, highlighting the gold embroidery, the symbols sparking a memory from a lifetime ago.

"I was beginning to think you were going to fold on my favor," Teach said.

"If the likes of you thinks so low of me, then my reputation among the good people is beyond repair." A distinctly feminine voice flowed from the hooded stranger. Her weathered hand appeared from beneath her cloak, snapping her fingers, sending a sparkle of dust fluttering in the air.

"You always were overly cautious, Mor. Would have thought you could have let your guard down amongst your own people," Teach chuckled. I peered around the crowded pub. Not a single person looked our way. Even the nosy barmaid found herself otherwise occupied, as though this stranger had somehow made us invisible in our dark corner.

"Times have changed. A fae can never be too careful," the woman said plainly. My heart raced in my chest. This was it. This is what I had been waiting years for.

She pulled down her hood, revealing features that were mature and stately, a classic beauty silhouetted in a spray of raven hair. But it was her eyes that caught my attention. Those amber eyes were timeless, a true mark of the fae.

"Take us back less than 200 years, and the Mor I knew flaunted whatever power she had. This realm could have been yours for the taking."

"Ah, to be young again. This realm wasn't ready for a woman to take the lead. It still isn't. But I'm not here to relive the glory days with you, Éadbard."

"Éadbard?" I asked, puzzling over yet another name for a man I thought I knew.

"I haven't heard that name in a long time. It'd be best to keep my given name quiet, or you may attract visitors that neither of us are prepared to deal with, my friend," Teach cautioned.

"The last time we spoke, I made it abundantly clear that you and I are no longer friends."

"I think I know where it is, Mor."

The woman's palms slammed on the table as she pushed herself up from her seat. "You haven't changed. And I told you before, I want nothing to do with it."

Teach grabbed her wrist in his iron grip. "As I see it, you still owe me a favor and I am here to collect. Or does your bond mean nothing?" The two stared at each other in a tense stand-off until Mor finally took her seat. They both seemed to be oblivious to my presence. But I couldn't let this opportunity pass me by.

"Captain, I… uh." I'd meant to confront him. Finally call him out as a fae, but the words stuck in my throat. Teach and Mor turned to stare at me.

"This is new," Mor started. "A human companion? Maybe I've misjudged you, Éadbard. Maybe you have changed. Never in all my years would I have expected you to bring a human into your confidences."

"He may be human, but believe me, he is more than what he seems. He's been beyond the veil." A wave of panic washed over me. How had Teach known? I'd made it a point to keep a tight grip on my secrets. The truth of Neverland and Peter Pan hadn't passed my lips. He'd alluded to the fact that he knew I was more than what I proclaimed to be, but the fact that he knew my secrets had alarm bells going off in my head. What else did he know? While my mind was in turmoil, Mor turned to look at me, her amber eyes boring into my soul with new curiosity.

"And yet you keep him in the dark?"

"Times may have changed, but trust is still something that requires blood, sweat, tears and absolute loyalty. That will never change. James here has finally proven himself. He also shares my desire to leave this miserable realm behind."

"You know that's not possible for you, Éadbard."

Teach slammed his glass of rum on the table. "Yes, it is! And that, my dear friend, is where you come in. The Heart of the Divine is within my grasp. I only need an invitation to Mag Mell, and I want you to arrange it for me."

The beautiful woman stared at Teach for a moment before she burst into a full-blown laugh. "This realm has affected you more than I realized! You have absolutely lost your mind."

"You owe me a favor and I need an audience with Manann. He knows where the ruby is."

"No, no. It'll never happen. Even if I get you an invitation, why would he tell you where it is?"

"That is for me to figure out. All I need is for you to return the favor I am owed, and I will gladly leave your shores. Never to return." Mor's gaze stared off into the fire, her jaw flexing as she contemplated his words.

I leaned over to Teach, trying to catch up on the entire situation. "What is Mag Mell?"

"Not what, but *where*. Mag Mell is the fae Otherworld. A place both of this realm and not of this realm," he said, doling out a ridiculously vague explanation.

"And by Manann, you can't mean the sea god?"

Teach chuckled, "One and the same. Manann is the king of Mag Mell. No one may enter without an invitation."

"Two days," Mor said coldly, interrupting my question-and-answer session. "In two days' time, sail into the western horizon. I will arrange the invitation. Go at your own peril. With any luck, Manann will keep you in the everlasting realm for eternity. Then your shadow will never again darken my doorstep."

I SWIRLED the rum in my glass, not entirely sure where to begin. The moment they had set the deal, Mor snapped her fingers and vanished before my eyes, leaving Teach and I to glare at each other in silence. Years of questions I'd been desperate to ask were now stuck in my throat. I'd been right. My pathway back to Neverland had been within arm's reach this whole time. And the worst part is that he'd known all along. I let the anger of that revelation simmer in my chest. I'd become complacent... And I knew the reason why.

*Love.*

I'd been falling in love with Kat for years. It had been so easy to immerse myself in her sweet distraction, and I'd let my ultimate goal slip out of my sights. Now I was finally seeing clearly. I had to focus because until I fed the demon within me, I couldn't move forward. As much as I hated to admit it, Peter Pan had broken me. I would never be able to give myself to Kat completely until the shattered pieces of my soul had been reforged.

"Don't act surprised, James. You've always known." Teach's words pulled me from my thoughts. He studied me as he stroked his beard.

"Suspected. That's very different from knowing."

"Indulge me. I know you've been across the veil. I know you're seeking a way back. Tell me, which realm holds sway over your heart?"

"I thought you knew everything?" I quipped before taking another swig of my rum.

Teach glared at me, crossing his arms over his chest, silently commanding me to answer.

"Neverland," I whispered. I hadn't said the word aloud in so long and it sounded like home as it rolled off my tongue.

"Well, I'll be damned. That speck of an island is little better than this realm."

"Anything is better than here. Plus, I have unfinished business there," I admitted.

"Ah, yes. Your vendetta."

"Thanks to you," I growled, "I've been denied what is owed for far too long."

"Vengeance is a dish best served cold, and with a glass of rum," Teach chuckled, shooting back another shot. "But mark me, once we get to Mag Mell and get the answers I need, I'll deliver Neverland to you on a silver platter."

"Tell me more. You want me to have your back? Then tell me about this ruby you're looking for?"

"The Heart of the Divine. I've been searching for it for centuries. Thanks to Katherine's visions, I finally know where to look."

"What's so special about it?"

"Truth is, I've been exiled to this realm," he started, and for the first time since I met him, he revealed a bit of his past. "I'm bound by magic to remain here for the rest of my preternatural life. But the ruby could change all of that. It will get me out of this hell."

"You still haven't answered my question. What is it?"

"It's a gemstone, but not just any gemstone. The ruby is ancient. Many believe it to be nothing more than a myth. Legend claims that it contains star dust from the first realm, placed there by the hand of the Divine. The power it contains... well let's just say that whoever possesses the ruby will have the entire cosmos in their hand."

"And this Manann, you expect him to simply tell you where it is?"

"Awe, James, you disappoint me. I know you're more cunning than that. I have a plan. I always have a plan."

# CHAPTER TEN
## -CHAOS-
### James

We sailed out at dawn the second day. Teach had been eager, almost manic, as he orchestrated the preparations for the voyage. He'd been an insufferable fuck. Worst of all, I hadn't had a single moment alone with Kat since we returned from Castlebar. When Teach wasn't on deck, ensuring his orders were being followed to the letter, he was in his cabin with Kat. I'd seen the relief in her eyes when I'd returned. I wanted to wrap her in my arms, tell her everything that had happened, but the best I'd managed was a grazing touch, my hand brushed hers as I passed by. I lingered just long enough to watch her green eyes disappear behind his door.

I'd upended my room when her throaty moans drifted down the hallway. I tried to remind myself that she had to put on a show for him. That this was all against her will, but the thought didn't give me any comfort. The idea of his hands on her, when she was supposed to be mine was almost more than I could bear. I let my rage grow as I paced the small space while the demon inside me stirred, reminding me that there was one person responsible for everything—Pan. It wasn't rational, but Pan was a familiar outlet for all the problems in my life. It was the path of least resistance since I couldn't take it out on Teach. As much as I wanted to gut him with my dagger for everything he'd done to Kat, I still needed him. I dropped my head in my hands. I felt sick, trapped, useless. Once my room was completely destroyed, I made my way to the bow to let the chilled ocean breeze cool my burning rage.

WHEN MY EYES popped open the next morning, they landed on a pair of well-oiled boots. Teach's imposing figure stood over me, gazing out at a horizon that was completely obscured by the thick mist that hadn't eased since the moment we'd set sail.

"Mornin'. Great day to travel to the Otherworld, don't you think?" Teach sounded unusually chipper. I grumbled as

I got to my feet. Trying my best to ignore the memory of Kat's moans that echoed in my head.

"How do you plan to keep the rest of the crew in the dark about all this? Or does it no longer matter?" I asked in a desperate effort to distract my mind from thoughts of him and Kat together.

"Pirates are a superstitious lot. Most of them already believe in the fae. Their stories will be seen as nothing more than embellished ramblings of drunken men," he answered, brushing off my concerns. "James," he started, clearing his throat.

"I don't think I ever thanked you properly," he paused, his gaze never leaving the obscured horizon. "For Katherine, I mean. She's been beyond valuable, and I would have overlooked her as nothing more than a lowly human. If it wasn't for her, I wouldn't be here now. She pulls at my heart in ways no woman has. Not to mention her pussy is just as sweet," he chuckled, and I felt my jaw clench as jealousy bubbled up in my chest. "But she's more than just a sweet piece of ass. She's the key, James."

"Key?" The simple word came out like a feral growl as I tried to hold my temper in check.

"The key to the ruby. The key to Manann."

"I'm sorry, Captain. I can't say that I follow?"

"Your race is evolving. Going through what's called the *tribulation* like every race before them. It's a painful rite of passage. Magic is growing, and some are born with more than others. Kat has been born with a particularly useful form of magic. Once she's touched you, not only can she peer into your future. She can see your secrets."

"Secrets? You mean she has more than just the sight?" My mind whirled with the idea. Kat had never explained her powers to me. But to be honest, I don't think I'd ever asked. It had always been a sore spot between the two of us. I knew she kept things from me, and I'd never gotten over it. But his words were like a hot knife of betrayal, sinking into my gut. She'd confided in Teach, and not me.

"Aye, one touch and she'll know," he continued. "That's why I need you to get her ready. She'll be coming with us to meet Manann. There's a dress I've been saving. One of the few things I still have from my life across the veil. It's from the First Realm and fit for a fae queen. I want Kat to wear it. If we're to make an impression, she'll have to be perfect. Go into my cabin and fetch it for her from the wardrobe. Make sure that she's put together."

"Aye, Captain."

"Oh, and James, make sure she knows to keep that sharp tongue of hers in check." He raised his brows as if to insinuate that if she ruined this mission, he'd take it out of her hide.

"The woman has a mind of her own, but I'll see what I can manage."

"She'll listen to you. She sees you like a brother after all these years."

I clenched my jaw shut to keep my smart mouth from

saying something I couldn't take back and asked a respectable question. "When will we arrive?"

"Whenever Manann deems it to be so. Could be an hour. Could be five days. Let's hope Mor worked her magic and got us in his good graces."

MY HEART RACED as the key turned in Kat's door. The moment Teach gave the order I'd been eager to get a moment alone with her. I had the elegant dress draped over my arm. I'd expected fine linens over thick skirts with petticoats and corsets, possibly even silks. But the dress I found hidden in Teach's wardrobe was unlike anything I'd ever seen. The silver and gold fabric shimmered in the dim light below deck, and I couldn't wait to see Kat in it. Even if it was a gift from Teach, she'd be wearing it for me.

Her expectant green eyes met mine when I pushed open the door and a smile lit her face when she saw it was me and not Teach.

"James," she breathed as she pushed up from the small desk in the corner. I closed the door quickly behind me, just before her tiny frame collided with mine. The feel of her in my arms, her body pressed against me, the sweet smell of her hair was rapture. It made every other thought leave me until there was only her. All my earlier feelings of betrayal and jealousy burned away with her touch.

"You're here. You came back for me," her words came out in a soft sob.

"Hey… shh. Don't cry." I pushed her back, tilting her chin up until her wet eyes met mine. "I'll always come for what's mine." She reached up on her toes and brushed her lips on mine, kissing me chastely.

"I was so worried. I thought I'd lost you. I thought that—"

"I'm here now, Kat. That's all that matters. And I have so much to tell you."

"What happened? Did he introduce you to Ruby?"

"Interesting fact; Ruby isn't a person, it's an actual ruby, and apparently Teach says—Sorry, I'm getting ahead of myself. I've found out something about the captain. I know you'll think I'm crazy, but hear me out. Kat—he's fae." I expected a look of confusion. I expected her to laugh at the absurdity of my confession, anything but the knowing look that flashed in her eyes before breaking my stare and biting solidly on her lower lip. "Wait," I raked my hands through my hair as the realization hit me. "You knew?"

"I… well, I didn't know exactly what he was. I mean, not until recently. I suspected he wasn't human," she confessed.

"You knew, and you never thought to tell me?"

"What was I supposed to say? I never thought you'd believe me."

"Goddamn it, woman! You've got an entire closet full of skeletons. Is it true that you can see a person's deepest secrets? Is that how you knew?" I challenged.

She sighed deeply, "Sometimes I do, but I cannot control what the visions show me."

I felt the muscles in my jaw tick as her admission sunk in.

"One moment you claim to love me, and the next you're keeping things from me that could determine our fate." Years of pent up longing, frustration, and jealousy boiled over.

"I've done no such thing!" she shouted, her hands digging into my chest as she shoved me away. "I've been meaning to tell you, and I would have. I was just waiting for the right time. And how dare you accuse me of keeping secrets when you're holding onto a graveyard worth of skeletons, *Jas*," she threw the old name in my face. A name given by my enemy. A name of a boy who I'd buried long ago.

"Never call me by that name again. That boy is lost to me."

"Isn't that what they say, though? Once a lost boy, always a lost boy?" Her words rattled the demon in my chest. Had she intentionally plucked those words from my mind knowing they would rip my heart out? How many secrets had she stolen from me over the years? My vision faltered as my hand whipped out, closing around her throat before I pinned her against the wall.

"Lies!" I growled, too loud for my own good. But I was lost. I couldn't rein in the demon that was starved for revenge. The absence of Pan made Katherine a vulnerable target for all of my rage. Her chest heaved against mine, her nails sinking into my arm as I glared at her. A look of shock flashed across her eyes before narrowing to slits.

"The difference between you and me, James, is that I have enough room in my heart to love you *and* all of your secrets. Apparently, I can't say the same for you." Her words only stoked the inferno raging within me and in the next instant, my lips were hard on hers. Our tongues clashing as my hand flexed around her neck while the other hitched her leg up. I wanted to claim her in that kiss. As though pure will alone would change the circumstances we found ourselves in.

"Mine! You. Are. Mine!" I growled, her mouth swallowing my words as she kissed me. My fingers dug into her soft backside, pulling her closer, but never close enough. She met me with a fervor of her own. Matching fire with fire. Her teeth sunk into my lip while her hands fisted in my hair. The silver tang of blood flooded my mouth. It was the taste of forbidden love that had been held back for far too long. Our needy hands roamed over each other. She cupped my hardness, and I groaned into her mouth. She was mine, and I'd denied myself for too long.

If it hadn't been for the pounding on the door I'm not sure if either of us would have been able to stop.

"James!" Henry's voice shouted as his fists rattled her door. "James! Captain's callin' for ya. Says it's time."

His words pulled me back to reality, and I managed to pull myself away. Kat ducked out from under my arms, cowering away from me.

"Kat, I'm sorry. Please. I didn't mean what I said. I just—"

"James, get your ass on deck. I don't think you want Captain to come looking for ya himself," Henry shouted as he continued to pound on the door. As much as I hated to admit it, he was right. Teach was the devil incarnate, but he was our only salvation at the moment.

"Yeah, I'm coming. Give me a minute," I called back.

"At your own peril, my friend," he responded before his footsteps faded away.

"We'll talk more once this is over. I think I have a plan for us," I said as I reached for the door. "And just so you know, I've always loved you, secrets and all. I'm the one whose failed. I've failed to be the man you could bare your soul to. If you'll only give me a chance, I promise I'll prove myself worthy of all of your demons."

When my boots hit the deck, the mist that had plagued us the whole voyage had swallowed up the entire ship. I could barely see the mast as I walked towards the castle deck.

"James, it's about damn time. You almost missed it," Teach called to me. His dark eyes looked wild as the mist swirled around him, caressing him as if it were sentient, taking weight of his character.

"Hold on to your hat's men!" he called to the crew. The ship lurched starboard, and the deck dropped out from below my feet. I grabbed for the railing as the world turned to chaos around me. Screams from the men mixed with the sound of groaning wooden planks, the ship protesting as we plummeted into nothingness. The mist blinded me. The wind whipped my hair, and the spray of water stung my face. I was losing my mind. One minute we'd been sailing solidly upon the ocean, and now we were falling through time and space. My heart raced in my chest. The only thing I could do was cower on the deck and hold on for dear life. The roar of wind drowned everything out, except for

Teach's sinister laugh, the sound of it chilling me to the bone.

When I was absolutely certain that I wouldn't survive, the *Queen Anne* jolted to a stop, sending me sprawling across the deck. The ship bobbed like a cork before settling on a calm sea. The mist that had engulfed us evaporated, leaving nothing but blue skies. I quickly composed myself, holding back the urge to run below deck and check on Kat. She was precious cargo. Teach would never have put her at risk. She was too valuable to his plan.

Unlike the rest of us, Teach stood firm on the deck. The only indication that he'd been affected at all was his wind-blown hair.

"Come, James, feast your eyes on the land of perpetual youth," he said. A wide grin spread across his face as his hand clamped down on my shoulder. A lush, green island nestled in sapphire waters, beckoning us forward. It instantly reminded me of Neverland and that certain ethereal beauty that did not exist in our realm. The air was warm and fragrant with the smell of jasmine on the wind as it filled our sails, delivering us to the harbor.

"Bring Katherine to me. Manann will be waiting for us when we reach the shore. It's time to let her work her magic."

# CHAPTER ELEVEN
## -FORBIDDEN-
### James

I was having a hard time keeping my gaze from lingering on Kat. She'd never looked so beautiful. Her hair was pulled back from her face and soft blonde waves cascaded down her back. The dress appeared to have been made of spun gold and silver, woven into a lacy pattern that revealed glimpses of her porcelain skin beneath. Her silver locket, the one she always wore, hung between her breasts, drawing my attention there. The fabric clung to her perfect curves, and she looked every bit of the fae that Teach wished she was.

A delegation of fae males and females, each one more

exceptionally beautiful than the last, waited to welcome us as we came to shore. An imposing man stood at the focal point of the group. His chiseled features were framed with chestnut hair that hung in waves around his bearded face. He wore no shirt, only a simple woven cape hung from his shoulders displaying intricate tattoos in patterns across his sculpted chest. His demeanor alone commanded respect, and I knew instantly, this was no man. This was the *god* we'd come to see.

"By my word... Éadbard, it's been far too long." His deep, melodic voice somehow soothed my nerves, easing the tension in my shoulders.

"Don't patronize me with pleasantries, Manann. If I was welcome in your realm, I wouldn't have had to go to such lengths to get an audience with you."

"Appears you haven't changed a bit, old friend," Manann chuckled.

"Old friend? If that is truly the case, then you'll extend your hospitality to me and my crew?"

"I would not have extended the invitation if it had been any other way. Please, come and enjoy the fruits of the island. Your men may find safe harbor here as long as they'd like."

"Your words are not lost on me. My men, but not me."

"I am bound by the laws, just as you are. I am stretching them thin by allowing you to be here now. Don't push me, Éadbard—or should I call you *Blackbeard*?" he mocked.

"You know as well as anyone else, the charges against me

were arbitrary," Teach scowled. Manann had obviously hit a nerve, and my curiosity flared. I'd been so wrapped up in my own affairs, I'd never gotten around to asking Teach what grave offense he'd committed to get himself exiled and now the question would plague me until I got an answer.

"Never the less, my hands are tied. I will give you sanctuary. Allow you a momentary reprieve. But know this; the clock is ticking. The longer you remain in a fae realm, the easier it will be for him to track you down," he cautioned. Who would be hunting us here? Who was this 'him' that the sea god warned of? I was getting the impression that even after all the truths that Teach had shared over the last few days, I was still ignorant to the danger he'd placed us in.

"Dually noted," Teach grumbled while he begrudgingly bowed to Manann.

"I see you've brought guests. It's been quite some time since we've entertained the lesser race. I speak for the entire island when I say, we are thoroughly intrigued."

"They may be lesser, but at least they produce some delectable specimens. Let me do the honor of introducing you to Katherine." Teach had placed a hand on the small of her back, pushing her toward Manann's imposing figure. His ice-blue eyes raked over my girl, not even attempting to hide the flare of desire as he lingered over her curves.

"It is my pleasure to welcome you to the Mag Mell. I am Manannan, Son of Lir, God of the Sea, King of the Otherworld. You may call me Manann." His formal titles rolled fluidly off his tongue. "I think the island will be a considerable upgrade to the realm you're accustomed to," he purred, reaching for her hand and placing a chaste kiss to her knuckles. I focused on Kat, trying to discern any change —any tell that she'd gotten the information that Teach was so desperate for. But she only smiled sweetly, showing no outward response as she curtseyed respectfully.

"Thank you for your warm welcome, Your Highness," she said sweetly. I could see it in his eyes, he was entranced by her.

"Come friends! Join me in the hall. We shall feast in honor of our guests." Manann tucked Kat's arm in his and turned toward the mainland, followed by his entourage. The crew looked to Teach for approval, and with a slight nod from the captain, they followed behind. I took a step forward, determined not to let Kat out of my sight when Teach's firm grip pulled me back.

"Keep your wits about you here. Evil tends to hide in the most beautiful of places. And do not drink the wine."

"I can't drink?"

"I'm giving you an order, boy! I expect you to obey without question. Now get moving. We mustn't keep Manann waiting."

I HELD my breath in anticipation as we reached an enormous structure rising from the lush landscape. I'd never seen anything so grand, not even in Neverland. A pair of massive golden doors embossed with woodland scenes and beasts glittered in the sun. The moment the doors swung open, my jaw dropped. It was hard to comprehend the enormity of the great hall. The ceilings rose so impossibly high that even clouds drifted among the stone columns. Silver trees lined the hall, swaying in a nonexistent wind. Their branches hung heavy with golden apples, but it was the music that drew me in the most. A melody that I could only assume was the sound of angels echoed off the cavernous walls. The beauty of it threatened to pull tears from my eyes. Several of the crew had done just that, falling to their knees and sobbing.

"Éadbard, join me at my table. You and your exquisite woman will entertain me for the evening," Manann ordered, before clapping his hands. The hall instantly became animated as nymphs and satyrs filtered in, clutching platters overloaded with food and bottles of wine.

I watched from a distance as Teach feasted with Manann. My girl—my Kat—sitting by his side. He spent the night in a gluttonous frenzy. Eating, drinking, and indulging in the nymphs that clustered around him. I watched from my place with the crew as a toxic anger began to fester within me.

He'd claimed to care for Kat and yet he had no problem molesting the two nymphs that currently sat in his lap right in front of her. And what's worse, it was clear that he'd given her to Manann for the evening. The selfish bastard would do anything to accomplish his task, no matter the cost. I questioned if perhaps I wasn't all that different. If I didn't have an agenda of my own, Kat and I wouldn't be in this predicament. The truth of that further worsened my mood.

And for a place of plenty, there was no friendly drop of mead or rum to ease my conscience—only the wine that I'd been forbidden to drink. Apparently, I was the only one who'd received those orders, because the entire crew hadn't had an empty cup all night. Each of them indulging in all the fruits of this *Otherworld*.

"Cheer up, my dear friend," Henry slurred as he sat down hard in the seat next to mine. "Can I tell you something?" he whispered dramatically in my ear. It was obvious the wine had gotten the better of my normally level-headed friend. His antics managed to pull a half-hearted smirk out from the corners of my mouth.

"I'm all ears, but I get the feeling you'd tell me even if I wasn't," I said sarcastically.

"Yoou… need to leave. Leave all of us behind. Especially Kat," he slurred.

"Excuse me?" I growled, my sensibilities evaporating with the turn the conversation was taking.

"I know you. You aren't… I mean, she's not… well. I know you can do better. Plus," he paused briefly before continuing, his words barely audible, "I think she likes it, what he does to her. Look," he motioned to Manann's table, "that's not the smile of a tortured soul." His whisper turned to a throaty laugh, and he sprung to his feet, stumbling back into the crowd of dancing fae.

I would have answered him with my fist, but I couldn't tear my eyes away from Kat as Manann offered her his hand. I couldn't deny that the coquettish smile on her face looked genuine. I'd seen her look at me that way hundreds of times. Henry had always been my confidante, someone who listened to me and saw past my flaws enough to be my friend. He'd never once admitted his distaste for Katherine in all these years. Why now?

I watched as Manann led Kat out of the great hall. My mind was at war. Henry's words bred new doubts, casting dark shadows over my relationship with her.

"James," Teach boomed and I jumped. His commanding voice intruding on my thoughts and catching me off guard. He had a beautiful nymph draped over each arm.

"Keep an eye on the men. I'll be preoccupied for the remainder of the evening," he grumbled, and the women nymphs giggled.

"Aye, Captain," I said flatly, but it hadn't mattered. His back was already turned to me, vanishing into the shadows with his trophies. This was supposed to be it, the brink of getting what I'd craved for so long, and yet the excitement I should have felt was gone, replaced by a rot of the mind, and my thoughts were deteriorating fast. Teach was whoring out my girl, and my best friend was undermining one of the few relationships that truly mattered to me. Sowing the seeds of doubt about the woman who gave my life meaning outside of my vendetta with Pan.

As the thought of him entered my mind, a flash of ruffled auburn hair caught my attention. I narrowed my gaze, focusing on a boy dressed in unkempt clothes with an oversized sword strapped to his back, weaving in and out of the crowd. My heart began to race as familiarity struck me like a bolt of lightning. I pushed back from the table, my chair kicking out from behind me. It couldn't be. But when the boy turned to look at me, there was no mistaking that cocky smile.

"Pan," I seethed, my hand shifting to my cutlass as I pursued him. The world around me blurred, my enemy finally within my sights. The demon in my chest roared, the sound deafening in my ears. I picked up my pace, weaving through the crowded hall, but I couldn't catch up. I began shoving the fae aside, my desperation growing with each beat of my heart.

I caught his condescending smile every time he turned to look at me, goading me into the chase. Everything felt wrong, but damned if I could stop myself from hunting him down. For a moment, I thought I'd lost him amongst the crowd, only to catch a glimpse of him sliding through a cast iron gate. I followed behind, finding myself in a moonlit garden. There he stood—my nemesis. My entire life's sacrifices had been leading up to this moment. His back was to me, standing on the edge of a massive fountain.

"Pan!" I called, stalking toward him. "I know you're a fucking coward, but the least you can do is turn and face me!" I was losing control, and the demon within me threatened to take over. The edges of my vision turned red with years of repressed rage. I closed the distance, reaching for him, needing to look into his eyes when I pierced his traitorous heart with my blade, but my hand ghosted through him. I stumbled forward, falling through the vision of my enemy. His form vanished into a cloud of mist that swirled around me and disappeared into the night sky.

"What the—" I spun around, desperate for it to be a trick. Desperate to find that I hadn't lost my grip on him after all these years of waiting.

"He speaks highly of you." I startled at the sound, instantly on guard as a dark figure emerged from the shadows.

"Who goes there? Show yourself!" I demanded, my adrenaline still churning through my veins. It was the sea god himself who stepped into the moonlight. "Manann? You know him? You know Pan? How is that possible?" I fired off the questions just as quickly as my calculating brain could produce them.

"Young James, am I right?" he asked, deflecting my questions as I appraised him with new eyes. "He tells me you're rare, a human with the heart of a true adventurer. A man who can see past what is on the horizon before you. For a human to be a traveler between the realms is rare indeed."

"Pan told you that?"

"Blackbeard. Although, I am familiar with this Pan you speak of. Another rarity of your kind. Curious that your fates are so ensnared with one another. Such a notion stimulates my mind. You see... I like to collect rare things. They intrigue me. Every time I think I've figured out the Divine's plan, something or someone finds a way to remind me just how small I am in the scheme of things," he mused.

"So, that was your little trick? How did you know of my connection to Pan? Were you trying to lure me here?"

"So many questions, it's unbecoming of a mortal," he tsked.

"Not just any mortal, as you so clearly pointed out."

"I knew I would like you, young James. A cunning mind will take you far. Now come, have a drink with me. Tell me of your adventures." He clapped my shoulder, pushing me toward an arched doorway at the back of the garden. The hair on the back of my neck prickled. My instincts told me I couldn't truly trust this man.

"I... I should probably get back to the crew." I fumbled with an excuse to walk away from the situation without offending a god in his own home.

"Just a glass of wine. You tell me your stories, and I'll share my tales of Neverland."

That was all I needed to hear. Teach had always been a means to an end. Maybe that end was leading me to Manann.

I let him lead me to what I assumed were his private chambers. A massive space dripping with opulence. Marble floors, ornate tapestries, an enormous fireplace set before a four poster bed that was large enough to sleep five full-grown men, and sitting there on that bed was Kat. She didn't take notice of our entrance, her glassy eyes locked on wisps of blue that danced around her head. A soft smile on her face, completely entranced by the glowing light.

"What's wrong with her? What have you... are those pixies?" I questioned as I stepped closer to her. The little blue wisps were actually delicate faeries, leaving a trail of water droplets around Kat's head as they encircled her.

"Water Sprites. Same family, just without all the dust." He waved it off as though it were nothing. "They go hand in hand with the god of the sea. They like her almost as much as I do. Don't worry, she's enjoying herself for a change," he added, trying to reassure me. "Leave her be and come indulge me with drink and conversation."

He led me to a table and a set of chairs positioned in front of grand bookcases that stretched a full twenty feet to the ceiling. I'd never seen so many books in one place. I'd taught myself to read from the moment I boarded *Queen Anne's Revenge*. While the crew plundered gold, I collected books.

"You read?" I asked. Surprised that a god would have any need of books.

"Yes. Another passion of mine. I find your Shakespeare to be far beyond his time, brilliance, I say. And what about you, young James?"

"Of course. Most men can't comprehend the notion, but knowledge is a weapon. Possibly one of the best ones to have in your armory."

"Truer words have never been spoken. Here, I've opened a bottle of wine. It's from my private collection. A superb vintage." I turned to the sound of liquid filling a glass.

"No, thank you. I cannot." I hesitated as I turned it down. I wanted nothing more than to drain the cup. My nerves were still on edge after seeing Pan—or the vision of Pan.

"Cannot or will not?"

"Is there a difference?"

"The difference is whether or not you're making the choice of your own free will. Are you owned, James?"

My teeth were clenched so tight that the muscles in my jaw ticked. "I am no one's property."

"And what about Blackbeard?"

I snatched at the proffered glass, ripping it from his hands, tipping it back and downing the entire contents in one gulp, desperate to prove that I was master of my own destiny. It was only afterward that I appreciated the divine flavor of the wine. I savored the lingering taste on my tongue. It was euphoric. A ball of warmth swirled in my gut and radiated across my body. It was as if I'd drank an entire bottle of rum in one sip. I could feel the corners of my mouth lift into a giddy smile. I felt fantastic. Better than I had all night. What the hell had I been waiting for? Teach had been holding out on me, the bastard.

"How's the wine?" Manann asked as he poured me another glass, a knowing smirk on his face.

"It's the best thing I've ever tasted in my life," I gushed. The euphoria continued to grow, burning through all ill will as my earlier reservations evaporated into the ether. I felt at peace with everything surrounding me and I was absolutely certain that Manann was the greatest god in all the realms.

"I see a kindred spirit in your curious soul. And I can't help but wonder why Éadbard has risked so much to come and see me?"

"Risk? Are you going to kill him?" The question no

sooner popped into my head before it spilled from my lips before I could even decide if it was a question I should be asking.

"Not me. He may be a heathen, but I cannot find it in me to condemn the man after all he's been through. But surely you know he is a hunted fae?" Manann looked at me curiously.

"The captain keeps his secrets close."

"And yet you follow him, no questions asked?"

"There is a reason for my silence. I have secrets of my own that I do not wish to draw attention to."

"This affair you have with Peter Pan?" he questioned.

"Yes. But that is not all." I could feel all my truths sitting in my throat, waiting to be spilled if he should ask of it. My inhibitions had completely abandoned me, and I was an open book.

"Do you know why Éadbard is here? What secrets are you keeping for the captain?" His captivating blue eyes pierced through me. I could feel the confession bubbling up inside me. Teach was here for information on the ruby. I wanted to tell him, because somehow I knew with all my heart that I could trust him.

"I have been keeping a secret. Blackbeard—" A ripple of nausea hit my gut and I paused. I wasn't supposed to relay this information to anyone, let alone the very god we intended to deceive. But I wanted to tell him. Something inside me yearned to expose everything that I had been hiding for so long.

"You can tell me, James. Whatever you tell me will remain between the two of us," he pressed, and I knew I was done for.

"He's in love with me," Katherine's feminine voice pulled me up short, clearing my swirling head and bringing me back to reality. "That's his secret. One that both of us would die to protect. I may be Blackbeard's property, but James is the one who owns my heart."

Manann's eyes grew wide. "By my word, James. Your story gets more interesting by the moment. I always did enjoy a good love triangle. Tell me, how do you stand it? To have your heart's desire ravaged by another man?" His question seemed sincere, but it dissolved the last remnants of euphoria from the wine. I clenched my fists, reminding myself that I was in the private quarters of a god, and I had to pick my words carefully.

"I have a plan for us," was the best I could manage and still sound cordial.

"And you prefer to torture yourself when you could simply find a more attainable woman to lavish with your affections?"

"Because this kind of love isn't a choice," she said, her eyes locking with mine. She was answering his question, but her words were for me. "He is my salvation. My North Star leading me home."

Manann clapped, "Love is a gift and a curse wrapped in an all-consuming package. The Divine works in mysterious ways. Should you escape your perilous predicament, do come back because that will be a tale worth telling."

Manann poured himself another glass of wine as though the night were just beginning when a keening wail pierced the quiet of the room. The sound was so intense my ears began to ache. Manann's attention shifted to the bed, as the once peaceful water sprites darted toward him. They swirled in a frenzy around his head, and a scowl replaced his easy-going smile.

"What are they doing? What's going on?" I asked, my hands still covering my ears from the sound.

"The water sprites are protectors of the seas around the island. There is an uninvited guest making his way to our shores."

"An uninvited guest? Who?"

"Uninvited, yes, but not unexpected. The bastard prince has come to seek his revenge."

# CHAPTER TWELVE
## -DECEPTION-
### Katherine

"Revenge?" James asked. It was a word he knew well. It was imbedded in his soul, and the mere mention of it rolling off Manann's tongue piqued his interest.

"Yes. Blackbeard has a shadow. One that will not stop until he's paid for his crimes. Coming here was an ill-advised decision, and now evil incarnate has washed up on my shores. Éadbard must be getting desperate." Manann stroked his beard, deep in contemplation as he paced.

"Are we in danger here?" James asked.

"Dorian, Son of the House of Einar—or as legend calls

him, the bastard prince—is relentless and anyone standing with Éadbard might as well have a black mark on his soul."

James turned to me, his blue eyes always heavy with the secrets we were forced to bear. "I must find Teach. I have to warn him."

I nodded slowly—reluctantly. I wanted to tell him no. I wanted to tell him we should let this bastard prince resolve our problems and take out Edward. Then we'd be free. We could sail off into the dawn of a new day with nothing but our love to guide us. But that wasn't Edward's fate. I'd seen it. At least I'd seen bits and pieces of it, and his destiny did not end here in Mag Mell. But for James and me? I couldn't be sure. Our fates were inextricably bound to Edward Teach, and we had no other choice.

MANANN LED us through an intricate maze of dimly lit hallways. The night's celebrations had died out and the only sound was our rushed footsteps echoing off the walls. James clung to my hand, keeping me close. His other rested on the pommel of his cutlass. It was a false sense of security. A simple blade would be useless against the magic of a fae hellbent on revenge. We were out of our league here. If we were too late, we'd be the ones to pay for Edward's poor decisions and it would likely cost us our lives.

"Éadbard!" Manann boomed, pounding his fists on a random doorway. "Wake up, old friend!" He continued until a muffled grumble responded and the door swung open. A bleary-eyed Edward greeted us with a scowl.

"Damn you, Manann. What's so important that you had to rouse me before the dawn?"

"I thought you might want to know that Dorian is en route to Mag Mell as we speak."

"Are you fucking with me?"

"Deception is a cloak you wear well, but I only speak the truth, and if you're not ready to meet your fate this night, then I suggest you make haste in your departure."

"I didn't think the fucker would find me so quickly."

"You are running out of time. His powers continue to manifest. It won't be long before even the mortal realms are no longer safe. You need to get your affairs in order."

"Katherine!" Edward barked at me. "I need the potion."

Months had passed since Edward had forced me to concoct an elixir for him. It had been inevitable that he'd discover I was an alchemist, and once he had, it was yet another of my talents that he exploited. He provided me with a mix of herbs I'd never seen before, and a scrawled out list of incantations to recite. He'd watched intently as I worked, correcting me when I said the strange words wrong, and I'd felt a momentary camaraderie between the two of us, but that had been short-lived. The moment the cork was set on the bottle of sparkling liquid, he stashed it away. When I asked what the potion was for, my question was met with a swift slap across the face and a reminder of my place as his slave. I'd never mentioned it again after that and neither had Edward until we'd reached the Otherworld.

I pulled the sparkling vial from its hiding place, tucked into my corset between my breasts. Edward grabbed the tiny bottle from my hands and disappeared back into his shadowed room, emerging with his coat and hat. James peered at me with a questioning gaze, but the only response I could offer was a shrug of my shoulders. I could see it in his eyes. He thought I had kept this from him. He always thought I was keeping secrets. Someday, I would show him. Prove that he was all wrong. But now, when our lives hung in the balance, wasn't the time for petty squabbles. If we didn't make it through this night, then none of it would matter.

WE FOUND DRAKE, Edward's first mate, in the main hall, passed out drunk from wine, the empty bottle still clutched in his hand. This had been the state of most of the crew we encountered along the way. They'd had a rude awakening. Both James and Edward dragging them to their feet with orders to return to *Queen Anne's Revenge* and get her ready to sail.

James reached for Drake, but Edward pulled him up short. "Leave him. It's better if he's out cold for this."

I watched curiously as Edward pulled his knife, cutting a small lock of Drake's hair, his hands steady and methodical, so as not to wake the snoring pirate. Without hesitation, he placed the greased hair into his mouth, popped the cork on the elixir, and swallowed it down like a shot of rum.

I stared at Edward, waiting for the secret of the potion to finally be revealed. But nothing was happening. Edward turned the knife on himself, slicing his palm in a quick jerk. Blood seeped from his clenched fist and dripped onto Drake. I felt a shiver run down my spine as I noted the dark, aubergine color of his blood, reminding me that he wasn't human. With each splatter of blood, the man on the floor changed. Slowly morphing into a figure I knew all too well. I stared in disbelief. Drake had transformed completely and now my eyes rested on a perfect doppelgänger of Edward, still snoring on the floor. I shot a look back at Edward, only it was Drake's eyes that stared back at me, blood still seeping from his clenched fist.

"Mighty fine potion we put together, don't you think, Katherine?" Drake spoke the words, but it was Edward's voice I heard.

"Edward? Is that really you?" I reached out to him, touching his face. Wondering if the façade would falter, but the transformation was perfect.

"Course it's me. Needed a slight distraction to ensure smooth sailing out of port. Drake here will do nicely. If only I didn't have to part with such a fine hat," he tsked as he laid it askew on the sleeping pirate, completing the ruse.

"You mean to leave him behind?" James questioned in shocked horror. "He's your first mate. You're offering him up as bait to save your own skin?"

"Don't look so surprised, James. I told you before that this world wasn't built for weak men. Besides, now that I'm in the market for a new first mate, I know the perfect man to fill the role. But only as long as you can prove you're worthy. So, are you ready, boy?"

MY HEART THUNDERED in my chest as we ran for our lives under the cover of darkness. The *Queen Anne* hadn't been anchored far, but it felt like we'd never reach the sanctuary of the ship. I was captured in a living nightmare where the air felt thick and branches pulled at my skirts, each step slower than the last. Never fast enough to escape what was coming for us. The wind had picked up and storm clouds gathered overhead. Thunder claps rolled over the island, each one louder than the last in an ominous crescendo to our seemingly inevitable demise. James still clung to my hand, pulling me along behind him. He hadn't cared if Edward saw, not this time. With death breathing down our backs, James was the only thing holding me together, bringing me hope. When it really mattered, he would be there, and the simple clasp of his hand in mine proved it.

Relief poured over me the moment we reached the *Queen Anne*, but it was a foolish notion to think our escape could be that easy. A howling scream rolled across the land, and a wave of energy blasted into the ship. The impact sent us sprawling, the splintered deck digging into my palms as I landed on my hands and knees. I was petrified. My hands shook so violently that I couldn't pull myself to my feet. Edward's hearty laugh broke the silence that followed.

"Apparently, the bastard prince didn't find our little spell very amusing. What I would have given to have witnessed it myself." Edward got to his feet; an amused look plastered on his face. "Don't sit there, get off your asses, and get this ship moving like your lives depend on it! James, take point as my first mate," he commanded.

"You heard him, lads! Lay aloft and loose the topgallants! Hoist away the topsail! Steady out the bowline! Haul men! Haul taut!" James settled into the role, shouting orders with a calm confidence. He was a natural leader, remaining stoic in the face of chaos, not a hint of fear in his eyes. "Katherine!" he called to me once the crew's orders were dished out. "I want you topside where I can keep an eye on you. If the ship goes down, I don't want you caught below deck." He reached for me, pulling me to my feet and leading me to the mainmast. "Stay here. The seas may get a bit rough. I'll tie you in place, but if the ships going down, cut the ropes and save yourself. I will find you." He placed a blade in my hand, lingering with his fingers fisted around mine. His blue eyes conveyed so much in that brief moment. And then he was gone, barking more orders as he went.

I trembled in place, thankful for the ropes around my waist to keep me standing. The men bustled around me, panic in motion. Edward stood at the helm, his gaze darting back to the coast as the ship pulled out of the harbor. I could see it in his eyes. We were cutting it close. Everything felt wrong. An arcane fear had crept into my chest, seizing my soul. I could feel him, the evil that was coming for us. I chanced a look back at the shoreline as it slowly drifted away. The wind whipped the trees and foliage, parting them perfectly for a dark figure to stalk out of the forest. When he reached the beach, his body disintegrated into a cloud of mist, rolling toward the sea. Everything went silent after that. The winds ceased abruptly. Our sails hung limp. Nothing more than a skitter of lightning darting across the sky.

"Do something!" I screamed, unable to remain quiet as my fear bled into panic. "He's coming for us! We have to move."

I tried to keep my eyes on the swirling mist, but all trace of him had disappeared. I frantically scanned the water as an overwhelming sense of dread filled me. Even the crew fell silent. The only sound was the creaking of the ship as it bobbed like a cork, completely stalled in our escape. Then the water began to boil, and a preternaturally handsome man emerged from the depths. His silken locks were so pale, they looked almost silver as they framed his face. He was every bit the shadow that Manann had described, dressed in fine black clothes. A pair of feathered wings, black as a ravens, stretched out behind him. He walked on water, stalking toward the ship, like a demon intent on dragging us to the pits of hell. Shrieks pierced the air as the crew saw the same fate coming for them. I couldn't pull my eyes from him. I knew this man. I'd seen him in Edward's future. But this couldn't be it. There was so much more to my visions. They had never failed me before, and yet I felt my confidence fading with every step he took toward the ship.

"Manann!" Edward bellowed. His voice piercing the dead silence that had settled over the sea. Manann stood on the shore with his entourage, all of them watching the spectacle. It was a plea. A desperate request. A clutch favor. My eyes fixed on the sea god, waiting to see his response. If he denied it, I couldn't see how my visions would ever come to fruition. It felt as though time slowed, each second dragging out as I waited for our fate to be decided. No potion or spell could save me now.

With a smirk, Manann pulled a curled animal horn from his robes, held it to his lips, and blew. The wailing moan hit my ears just as the wind filled our sails, pushing the ship forward with great speed as an unnatural fog swallowed us. The last thing I remember was the thundering howl from the bastard prince as we slipped from his grasp, and the ship plummeted into its dark descent back to the mortal realm.

I STOOD at the window in the captain's quarters. My arms still tucked in around me, waiting for something to rise from the sea and pull us down to the death we'd narrowly escaped.

Edward sat at his desk, pouring himself a healthy ration of rum, while James paced the room. Once it was clear that we weren't about to be devoured by evil, James had demanded an audience with the captain. His anger was boiling just below the surface, a coiled snake waiting to lash out. Edward had kept us all in the dark about the bastard prince, and we'd almost lost our lives because of it. All for the sake of this ruby.

"Alright, James. Say your peace. The tension radiating off you is giving me a headache."

"You owe me answers!"

"I don't owe you anything. The sooner you realize that the world doesn't owe you a damn thing, the better off you'll be."

"Your secrets could have gotten her killed!" James snarled, and Edward raised a brow in response.

"But she didn't die, so your point is moot. And furthermore, do you ever listen to what I say? I've told you before, never let a woman distract you. Had she died, it wouldn't have mattered. I would simply find another way to get what I want." His words cut deep, deeper than I wanted to admit. I'd been Edward's concubine for years, and somehow I'd convinced myself that I was more than just a useful slave. His callous words brought me back to the reality that was my life. I was disposable. A warm place to put his cock until I was no longer useful. A lump formed in my throat. This couldn't be my life. I'd let him use me for too long, but I was done rolling over for him.

"Well then," James started. "Maybe I'll talk in a language you understand." He pulled a knife from his belt, rolled up his sleeve, revealing a perfect scar of a skull and crossbones. "I'll cut out my loyalty to you and leave you to rot on this ship until the bastard prince disposes of you."

Edward chuckled to himself. "How does it feel to finally grow a pair of balls?"

"Don't fuck with me, Edward. I want to know everything about the ruby. I want to know your connection to this bastard prince, or I walk." James held the blade tight to his arm and blood began to pour over the scar, a crimson trickle running down to his wrist.

"I'll tell you what you need to know. But don't you ever try to blackmail me with your loyalty again," he growled. "Or you'll find that blade hilt deep in your chest."

The two men glared at each other for a long moment. And for the first time, I could see that James had outgrown him. He wouldn't last long as Edward's subordinate. The man was destined to be a leader in his own right. He was a growing tempest that wouldn't be contained.

"Sit down, James. Have a drink." Edward poured out another glass of rum, pushing it toward him. James pulled up a chair and sat across from Edward.

"Now talk," James barked.

"Once upon a time," he began theatrically, pausing to take another swig of rum. "I served the King of Patreyus. The great king of the first realm. I'd worked my way through the ranks, and I was next in line to command the entire fleet.

That's why I was personally chosen for the assignment. You see, the king likes to indulge in forbidden pleasures, but he'd gotten careless and one of his mistresses managed to slip away and bear a child. Not just any child. A bastard child born with his power. One that could match his own—a direct threat to his kingdom. I was the unfortunate soul tasked with cleaning up his little indiscretion. I was ruthless in my pursuit. Years of my life wasted. When I finally hunted them down, I dispatched the mother without a second thought. I'd disposed of my fair share of whores, so it was nothing. But when a silver-haired boy stared up at me with innocent eyes, I hadn't been able to kill him for the crime of being born. A regret that I carry with me every day."

"That boy is now the bastard prince that hunts you?" James asked.

"One and the same. He's already taken my life once. Sparing him that day cost me everything. The king is not a forgiving man, and I was exiled from all fae lands as punishment for my failure. Now the bastard I spared all those years ago is dead set on ending my life as payment for killing his mother. But I'm not so easy to kill and I have a plan."

"That's where the ruby comes in?" I asked, putting the pieces together.

"Aye, the ruby is my salvation."

"How? What does it do?" James asked.

"Everything. It's known as the Heart of the Divine. Legend

has it that when the Divine created the original realm, they breathed life into every corner. A realm of unparalleled beauty, teeming with the most magnificent of creatures, ones created in their own image. The magic of the Divine beating at it's core. Yet as eons passed, the harmony of their creation began to crumble. The magic corrupted them, and they grew reckless and greedy. Harnessing the divine energy for their own ambitions, they sowed discord and devastation across the land. The realm descended into darkness.

In a desperate moment of regret, the Divine destroyed the realm. As a reminder of their betrayal, they extracted the stardust, the very essence of the magic that had been so ruthlessly abused and sealed it within a perfect ruby. It contains an entire realm's worth of magic. Once I possess it, I'll be free to travel between realms once again. No more faerie dust required. The king's exile would become irrelevant and all who oppose me, will cower at my feet."

"No faerie dust, you say?" James asked, fixating on the most mundane part of all that Edward had said.

"It is the key to freedom, my boy. And now, if you're quite finished, I believe Katherine has some valuable information to share, don't you, darling?" Both of them set their eyes on me, as though they finally realized I'd been in the room this whole time. "Come, tell me what you've seen. I want to hear what it was like to be in the mind of a god." Edward patted his lap, beckoning me forward. I balked for a moment. The inclination to defy him reared up within me for the first time in years. I walked slowly to him, sitting on his lap as I contemplated my next move.

"Now, sweetness, where is Manann hiding my ruby?"

"A remote island in the Tierra del Fuego," I said stoically. It wasn't a lie, but it wasn't the complete truth, either. I knew what lurked in the depths guarding the treasure of all treasures, and without that knowledge *Queen Anne's Revenge* would find her final resting place at the bottom of the ocean. With everything that had happened, it no longer mattered to me if I went down with her. As long as I could escape the prison I found myself in.

"Hmm, leave it to that bastard to hide it amongst the most treacherous waters. But that's no matter. We will prevail. James, we have our bearing. Get yourself topside, rile the crew and set the wind at our backs. I'll join you on deck once Katherine's helped me to relieve a bit of tension." Edward's grip tightened around my waist and my skin crawled. I could hear it in his tone, he was feeling reckless, and he'd be taking it out on my body. James' gaze met mine for only a moment, but I could see the anger flaring in his forget-me-not eyes. We were skirting a very fine line and the longer we walked it, the more blurred the line became. We were at our breaking point, and even as James walked out the door, I knew that this may be one of the last times he left me in Edward's hands.

# CHAPTER THIRTEEN
## -TRUTH-
### James

**M**uffled moans and giggles echoed down the passageway. The sound of Teach molesting my girl in the next room had me reeling with anger. If I didn't know better, I would have thought she was enjoying herself. My stomach was sick. My knuckles ached as I clenched my fists. It was all I could do to stop myself from breaking down his door and whisking Kat away from here, once and for all. If I were a better man, I would forget my vendetta against Pan and rescue Kat from this hell I'd brought her into. But no matter how much I loved her, my need for revenge was my first priority. With Pan still out there, she would always be second.

I made my way to the main deck to get some fresh air and clear the sound of their sins from my ears. I couldn't continue like this. I was going to snap. I had to get my hands on that ruby and take Kat with me to Neverland. It was the only way we would be free to love each other. Together, we could take Neverland for our own. Live out our lives in the paradise that was the island. I allowed myself to fantasize about the future while gazing off into the horizon. The inky sky was peppered with twinkling stars. Somewhere out there, the veil was waiting for my return. A hypnotic dance of moonlight reflected off the rippling surface of the sea. I would never tire of seeing it. It always seemed to soothe my weary soul. But tonight, the waters seemed eerily calm—too calm for my liking. The universe was preparing for something.

"James," Henry pulled me from my thoughts. "Captain's calling for you."

"Aye. Bastard's always been a minute man." I sighed and Henry chuckled, nodding his head in agreement. "I'll make my way down to his cabin. Have you ever seen the sea so calm? Nary a swell to be seen."

"It is… unusual. Perhaps a gift from Manann?"

"That's what I'm afraid of, my friend. The gods are a manipulative kind. Keep your eyes on the water. Report to me if anything seems off."

I OPENED the door to Teach's cabin only to find him and Katherine still lying in bed. His arm wrapped around her waist in a cuddle. I had to remind myself to breathe. It was all for show. Soon we would be free of his desires. Soon she would be in my bed. In my arms."

"James, take Katherine to her room. Clean her up, see that she is fed and put to bed," Teach ordered, pulling back the sheet to allow Katherine out of his embrace.

"Aye, Captain."

She quietly padded across the room. Her chin held high, confident in her nakedness with a smile hiding in the corners of her sinful mouth. I could feel my heart pounding in my chest, begging for me to do something. Anything. A red welt in the shape of a hand had bloomed on her porcelain skin. A reminder of where his hands had been. I gritted my teeth, forcing myself to remain silent, painfully flexing my jaw. I took a cleansing breath and followed her silently down the passageway.

"Get dressed," I demanded. Opening the door to her room, unable to hide my disdain. "I'll be back with some food."

"James?" she questioned delicately, sensing my unease.

"Not now, Katherine." I spoke the words quietly and closed the door behind me. I didn't enjoy being short with her, but I needed a minute to process what I'd seen. My anger wasn't with her, and I wouldn't subject her to more punishment. It was becoming virtually impossible for me to sit back silently and watch Teach have his way with Katherine. It was time to tell her about Neverland. Tonight, we would plan our escape.

I PLACED her plate on the desk and promptly locked us in the room. No one would question why her door was locked and Teach would be down for the night. I had finally managed to concoct an elixir that I was mostly confident wouldn't kill him and slipped it into his bottle of rum. The night cap would do more than simply ease his tensions, leaving us with a window of opportunity.

She had pulled on a gauzy shift and her pert nipples commanded attention. I could take her right here, and no one would be the wiser. I wanted to mark her, to claim her. Show the world she was mine. But to have her all to myself I needed to get her away from Teach. I pulled up the chair sitting across from her and shifted my gaze out the porthole. I needed to stay focused. I took another cleansing breath before looking back at her beautiful face. "I'm sorry I was short with you. Seeing you with him..." I trailed off, shaking my head. I didn't need to give her excuses for my actions. I was here to convince her to leave.

"I'm sorry you have to bear witness to his desire. Seeing

you like this breaks my heart." Katherine reached across the desk and grabbed my hand. "My body may be with him, but my heart belongs to you." I pulled her hand to my lips and placed a kiss upon her knuckles. Allowing her words to soothe my anger. "What was it you wanted to discuss?" she asked. Her brows drawing together in concern.

"In all my years, I haven't told a soul about my past. It's time I shared my story with you."

"I've seen things in my visions. I know your past is clouded in darkness, but it's also full of beautiful, otherworldly places."

"The place you have seen is called Neverland. Have you heard of it?" I asked, knowing the answer would be no.

"Neverland?" she pondered. "No, I don't think I have."

"It's a beautiful place, far away from here. Beyond the veil of time and space."

She looked at me with wide, expectant eyes, ready to lift the shadows from my secrets.

"I think you're going to need a drink." I poured her a heavy cup of rum and pushed it towards her. "Neverland, though small, is a lush island full of adventure. There is a sprawling forest, a mermaid lagoon—"

"A mermaid lagoon?" she exclaimed.

"Yes," I chuckled. "The lagoon is fed by a large waterfall, and beautiful mermaids call it their home."

"I've only ever read about mermaids. I thought they were mythical creatures."

"I can tell you they are quite real and though they are undeniably beautiful, they can be nasty creatures."

"Nasty? Really?"

"Give them the chance and they'll lure you in to the deep with their beauty, and when you least expect it, while distracted in their seduction," I reached under the table and grabbed her ankle, causing her to squeal, "they drag you through the depths to a watery grave. I've seen it happen with my own eyes."

"That's not nasty, that's diabolical." She chuckled, crinkling her nose at me. "Are there other mythological creatures in Neverland?"

"Everything in Neverland is what *this* realm would call mythological. There are the nymphs and satyrs. They are the native Neverlanders. There are gnomes, who are mostly tailors. Sex-obsessed pixies, a variety of beasts, and of course —Peter Pan, the boy who never grows up," I spat his name as if speaking it aloud put a foul taste in my mouth. Talking about Neverland for the first time in years had me feeling nostalgic. There was a hole in my heart that could only be filled with that damn island. It was my home, and I missed it dearly. But it also fanned the ever burning vendetta in my soul.

"The boy who never grows up? Does this Peter have auburn hair?

I could feel my expression change as her question caught me off guard. She must have seen him in her visions. "Yes," I hissed. My brow furrowed, and I shifted my gaze back to the porthole. "This is where things get complicated." I sighed. "When I was a young lad, I was taken to Neverland by Peter Pan. He promised me Utopia in exchange for my friendship. A magical wonderland with no adults to spoil our fun. The only rule to this arrangement was that I simply never grow up."

"That's a peculiar stipulation."

"In the beginning, I didn't think it was. He was my best friend—my family. But that all changed when I couldn't stop my body from aging."

"How does one stop aging?"

"You see, that's the problem. I am but a mere human. I can't stop. Time moves slower in Neverland. But for Peter, it has stopped completely. He doesn't age, ever."

"Is he human?"

"I don't know what he is. He looks human, but he is inexplicably connected to the island."

"A changeling?" It was a logical connection to assume Pan was fae, but Peter was something altogether different.

"He claims as a baby he flew from his nursery to Kensington gardens in London, England. Where he was raised by birds and faeries."

"Wait! He flew?"

"We all can, with the help of some faerie dust."

"James, I have seen some things in my life that are beyond explanation, but it's impossible for humans to fly. He must be fae."

"Oh, my dear, nothing is impossible." I reached into my pocket and pulled out the vial of faerie dust. I rolled the bottle between my fingers, entranced by the way the dust glimmered in the candlelight. "This is faerie dust. I have been holding on to this vial for many years in hopes I could find more and make my way back to Neverland." It was now or never. I had to convince Kat that I was telling the truth. I popped open the vial and smeared a small amount over my cheek. Just enough to lift off for a moment. I closed my eyes and thought of sweet, sweet revenge. I felt the floor part from my feet and opened my eyes as Katherine gasped, wide eyed in disbelief.

"James, you… you're—"

"Flying, yes." I circled around her in the air before dropping back down. I never had gotten used to the feeling. It was unnatural, and I preferred keeping my feet on the ground.

"Can I try?"

"Someday I'll teach you how, but right now, this tiny vial is all I have. In all my years, I haven't been able to find another source. We are going to need it when we get back." The words were out of my mouth before I could stop them.

"When we get back?" Katherine asked, confused. "What do you mean?"

"I have spent years here in this realm, looking for a way back. Peter exiled me from my only home with nothing but a festering wound and the clothes on my back. A young man with no knowledge of how this realm works. Left to die on the street like a filthy rat. I will get my revenge on him or die trying."

"And you want me to go back with you?"

"Yes. I want us to be free to love each other. It's time, Katherine. I can not continue to watch as Teach defiles you and uses you for his own personal gain. Together, we can defeat Pan and rule all of Neverland. We will slow the hands of time and live beyond our years in paradise. No Teach, no Pan."

"And how are we supposed to get back to your Neverland? You just said you couldn't find more faerie dust."

A sinister smile spread across my face. I didn't need to answer the question.

"The ruby." She nodded quickly, putting the pieces together. "You want the ruby for yourself."

"That ruby is our redemption. We must find a way to steal it from Teach and use it to make our way across the veil, back to Neverland. We just need to figure out exactly how it works."

"In the Otherworld, when I connected with Manann, I saw things. I think the ruby is intuitive. I'm sure once I get my hands on the real thing, it will unveil itself and its abilities."

"So, does that mean… are you going back with me?"

She smiled and nodded yes. I swear in that moment I felt my heart skip a beat. All my years searching and living under Teaches thumb were about to pay off. I could finally see a way back to Neverland, and Katherine would be at my side. I reached across the desk, pulling her face towards mine, and sealed her words with a kiss. "I love you," I whispered softly against her lips.

"I love you too. But, James, if we are going to do this, we're going to need a solid plan. Teach won't give up the ruby. He has been searching for it for years. Don't forget that he views it as his own salvation." Katherine's words pulled me back from my thoughts. She was right. Teach would kill anyone who stood between him and the ruby.

"It won't be easy, but nothing worth having ever is."

"There is one fatal flaw in Teach's plans." Katherine smirked. "Something I've kept hidden from him."

"A fatal flaw?" I questioned, stroking my beard. "I like the sound of that."

"Guarding the island, lurking beneath the depths, is a massive tentacled monster unlike anything I have ever seen."

"A kraken?" I had only heard of sightings in the cold waters off the coast of Norway. But what better way to guard a magical relic than an unexpected sea monster? If she had indeed seen a kraken, we were in for one hell of a battle. Few men lived to tell the tale, even fewer came back whole.

"I don't know what it's called, but it looks like a giant squid. It will be the *Queen Anne's* demise."

"That's definitely a kraken. Will *we* survive this attack?" I asked, hoping she had seen the outcome.

She shrugged her shoulders. "I have seen things that haven't yet come to pass. The future is fluid. Nothing is set in stone. It will be a bloodbath. The likes of which we have never seen."

"Then I can assume there is a chance. Knowing an attack is coming gives us the upper hand. We will be ready and waiting. That will be our opportunity to break free from Teach. He'll be distracted with keeping the *Queen Anne* above water. We'll jump ship and make our way to the island, snatch up the ruby before Teach can even get his grubby hands on it."

"What if we fail?"

"Then we shall perish and spend eternity together in the afterlife. At least we can say we tried."

"Here's to breaking free of Teach's rule." She raised her glass in a toast. "To eternal love."

"To us!" I took a celebratory swig of rum and stood up, pulling Kat into an embrace. For once, the future had me in its favor, and I was excited to see what it would bring. I lifted Kat's chin and kissed her gently. A promise of things to come. "The future is ours, my love."

"James," she spoke softly. "Were there others? I mean, boys like yourself, in Neverland?"

"There were others, but I was the first. He called us his 'Lost Boys.'"

Katherine's eyes lit up recognizing the term. "Once a lost boy, always a lost boy," she whispered the words as more puzzle pieces fell into place.

I paused, remembering my small family. "I don't know what became of them. They too, would have someday grown up." We were innocent children lured into a fairytale. We were happy for a time. Until the inevitable happened. "I imagine he did the same to them."

"Then we go for us *and* them. Together we will stop Pan."

I didn't think I could be more in love with Katherine Hawkins, but with those five words I fell even harder.

# CHAPTER FOURTEEN
## -SUFFERING-
### James

I awoke with a start, instantly on alert. A red apple coming into focus in my direct line of sight. It sat, curiously, on my desk. A pop of color in my otherwise drab room. Strange. I hadn't remembered any apples being among the rations. A gift maybe? Teach's feeble attempt to compensate for his insufferable behavior as the days at sea dragged on. He scrutinized everything, and his paranoia was becoming difficult to manage. I sat up cautiously, looking around, but the tiny room was quiet, dimly lit by the predawn light filtering in through the porthole. I sighed. It was another day at sea, and I was beginning to think I was going mad. The days stretched on in endless monotony. Even with favorable winds, there was no quick way to sail from the northern Atlantic to the bottom of the Earth at Cape Horn. My new role as Teach's first mate spared me from the grunt labor of sailing, but I found myself subject to an entirely different sort of hell. I'd spent most of my days pouring over maps with Teach. Watching while he relentlessly interrogated Katherine, pushing for more information. She said the island we were looking for sat south of the Tierra del Fuego, but not a single map showed an island where she insisted it should be.

"You bitch! You best not be lying to me!" I heard the captain's shouts down the hall, and I was instantly in motion, barreling toward his cabin. I busted through the door to find Teach with his hands around Kat's neck, shaking her like a rag doll. Seeing her like that triggered the predator within me. My vision flashed red, casting everything in a haze as instinct took over. Within moments, the dagger was in my hand. Luckily, I had the wherewithal to use the hilt rather than the blade. I slammed the butt of my knife into his shoulder, deadening his arm instantly. The blow broke his hold on Kat, and she sunk to the floor in a heap. Teach whirled on me, a feral look in his eyes. I was so consumed by rage that I couldn't control my fist as it connected with his jaw. He stumbled backward, a hand going to his bloodied lip.

"What the fuck, James!"

His words brought me up short, clearing my vision and

bringing me back to reality. "Captain, I'm—my apologies. I don't know what came over me. I thought maybe she'd pushed you too far, and I wanted to save you the regret of killing her when we're so close," I lied. But I knew it wouldn't be enough to save me from his wrath. The demon in my chest purred. It had been worth it. It had felt so good when my fist met his jaw and the high of getting some semblance of revenge for Kat was heady.

"You fucking bastard." The look on Teach's face was lethal, and he closed the distance between us in two long strides. I doubled over when his ringed fist rammed into my gut. This was my punishment. If I had been any other member of the crew, I would have hung from the mast or been flung overboard. But being that I was first mate, Teach was forced to punish me privately. I righted myself just in time to take a blow to the face. My head whipped to the side, blood spraying from my mouth. I could hear Kat cry out, her sobs filling the room, but it did nothing to deter him. I stood again to face him, taking my punishment with my hands fisted at my side. I heard the sickening crunch as my nose broke with his next punch. This time, the room spun, and I fell to the floor.

"You ever get between me and my property again and being my first mate won't save you from an agonizing death," he growled and kicked me solidly in the gut. I coughed and spluttered. Blood poured from my nose, but I managed a weak "Yes, Captain." Before he walked back to his desk and sat down.

"Katherine, get me something to clean my hands," he ordered, and she jumped, bringing him a handkerchief in quick order. "Now, to settle this once and for all," he said, cleaning my blood from his rings. He pulled a small vial from his belt and set it on the table. "Drink that. You won't be able to hide your little white lies from me anymore." He gestured again to the bottle of milky white fluid. I could see the color drain from her face. Teach had been forcing her to concoct any number of elixirs and poisons when she wasn't warming his bed, and now she would become a victim of her own creation. She glanced at me, and he slammed his fist on the table. "Don't look at him. Look at me! He can't save you, darling. Now pick up that vial and drink." She grabbed the tiny bottle in her shaking hands. I wanted to stop her. What if she couldn't keep our secrets? My heart pounded in my chest, but there was nothing I could do. Teach was right. I couldn't save her from this. I began mentally preparing myself. There was a distinct possibility that one of us wouldn't be leaving this room alive.

Kat pinched her eyes closed and swallowed the truth serum, gagging and gripping at her throat as it went down.

"I like to see you choking. Later, I'll replace that potion with my cock, and you'll choke on it until I give you permission to breathe." He sneered at her as she doubled over in a coughing fit. "Tell me, have you been honest with me about the location of the ruby?"

"Yes, sir!" she sputtered.

"And the location of the island?"

"I swear," she cried. "It's south of the Tierra del Fuego. It's not showing on your maps, but I promise it's there."

"Good girl. Is there anything else about the ruby that Manann told you?"

She paused for a moment. "No," she breathed, and it looked painful to get the word out. I tried to hide the look of relief that washed over me. She'd managed to keep the secret of the Kraken from him. It was our one and only wild card and she'd overcome the potion and fed him the lie that kept our plans intact. Maybe her powers were stronger than even Teach realized.

"And do you love me?" he asked condescendingly, and I waited with bated breath, my heart seeming to still in my chest.

"Yes," she whispered, equally as pained, tears pouring from her eyes as she said it. An obvious lie she'd fed him to placate his ego. I breathed a sigh of relief. Teach chuckled to himself, low and sinister.

"Leave my sight. We're done here. Seeing your tears usually excites me, but today they just seem pathetic." Teach snagged a bottle of rum and focused his attention on the maps before him, ignoring her completely. "James, you stay. We have work to do if we hope to navigate these waters successfully."

I KNOCKED GENTLY before turning the key and cracked the door open. "Kat? May I come in?" I peeked into the darkened room, only to find Katherine still in her bed. She'd been sick since Teach had forced her to drink the truth potion. Most days it had taken every bit of encouragement to even get her moving. She huffed at me, flipping over, turning her back to me. I let myself in, closing the door behind me. I refused to let her go through this alone. "I brought you some tea. I managed to get you some peppermint and ginger. Well, Henry got them for you, but I added honey and a splash of rum for good measure. It should help you feel better," I spoke softly while I set the steaming cup on her bedside table.

"I'm not much for company right now," she said listlessly.

"I promise I won't keep you. But I had to tell you... it's been eating away at me. I need to tell you I'm sorry."

"Sorry?" she questioned as she finally turned to face me.

"Yes, I'm sorry. I'll never forgive myself. I have failed you so many times. I know I am not a good man. I don't proclaim to be—"

"James, you—"

"No, let me say this," I insisted. "I should have protected you from Teach. I should have kept you safe, and yet here you are, suffering because of him yet again. And I stood by and watched."

"We both agreed that we'd continue the ruse until we had the ruby. That was the plan. You were sticking to the plan."

"At what cost? I'm supposed to protect you. Aside from

loving you, it's the one job I have. I have failed miserably. I'm not sure I can even call myself a man."

She smiled at me, and the look of it warmed my heart. She hadn't been smiling enough lately, and it was all my fault.

"Have I ever told you how much I love you, James?" The words were sweet music to my ears.

"I don't believe I've heard that story yet," I said playfully, breaking the somber mood in the room. "But you have my rapt attention. Please tell me, milady, exactly how much do you love me?" She giggled, and I leaned in to kiss her, but the moment my lips touched hers, the hinges on her door creaked in protest only moments before the door swung wide and Teach stood in the doorway. I pulled away from her a mere heartbeat before he caught us.

"Ah, there you are. James, you've been noticeably absent from your responsibilities topside."

"My apologies, Captain. I was simply seeing to my duties with Katherine, and I'll be on my way." Teach peered over my shoulder, his eyes roaming over Kat, who was still in her shift.

"Doesn't look like you've accomplished much. She isn't even out of bed yet. I should reassign her care to another member of the crew. Looking after the token whore is beneath your status."

"It's fine, Captain. I can manage. I'll be finishing up here in a moment."

"No matter. She might as well stay in her shift. Less work for me to strip her down."

"But, Captain, she isn't well."

Teach cocked his head at me. "Since when is that any of your concern?"

"I am your first mate. It's my job to look after all of your assets. As well as pointing out when you're being unnecessarily reckless with said assets. She is the only link we have to finding that island. If you break her, then everything is lost."

"Is that so? You are looking out for my best interest?" He said before he pulled an apple from a pouch at his belt and regarded me with a suspicious look. My eyes caught on the apple in his hand, reminding me of the one in my room. He slowly sunk his teeth into the skin, taking a bite, the very symbol of Eve's betrayal. Was it a warning? It couldn't be. The fae gave no credence to the religious tales of mortal men, and yet I couldn't dismiss the possibility that he was manipulating me with a symbolic display. A veiled acknowledgment he knew of our affair? Or was my conscience playing tricks on me?

"Yes, Captain," I seethed.

"Captain, that right there is the word I'm looking for. Last time I checked, I am still the captain, and you are the first mate. I make the rules. You follow them." He took another bite of his apple, drawing out the moment, waiting to see if I'd push him further, but I kept my mouth shut. "If you had the crew's best intentions at heart, then we should throw her overboard, lest she gets the rest of the men sick."

"If you want to find the ruby as badly as you say you do, then that's an order you'll never give. At least not until you've recovered the gem." I called his bluff rather than show my hand, because the moment I let on that there were any feelings between Katherine and I, that would be the last confession I made.

"Seeing that we both agree that I'm the captain, the ship needs a good swabbing this morning. See to it that all the decks are shining before you start your normal duties for the day." He smirked as he handed down the order. It was meant to humiliate me in front of the crew, and it would send a clear message that the captain and I were at odds. One thing about pirates, a majority of them were cutthroats and would be quick to stab me in the back if it meant a raise in ranks for themselves.

"And, Katherine, you best drink up that concoction of twigs he's brought you and be the picture of health when I come for you this evening." He glared at her, and there was no missing the threat in his tone.

I WIPED my brow as I rested against the foremast, still clutching the mop in my blistered hand. The seas ahead remained quiet.

Too quiet. The calm before the storm I knew was coming for us. Several among the crew had smirked and snickered at my expense. Purposefully spilling things on the deck after I'd cleaned it. Worst of all were the numerous rotten apples I'd found littered about the ship. The mundane sightings wreaking havoc on my sanity. I'd questioned the crew and not one man could account for where they came from.

I took mental notes about who I could and couldn't trust on this ship. Henry had been noticeably absent. I'd have to seek him out once things had settled and get a handle on all the talk amongst the men. Things were tenuous, and tempers were short. I only had to hold it together for a little while longer.

I turned; my attention diverted by a commotion behind me. The boisterous chatter of men swelled, like a growing storm on the horizon.

"String him up!" one shouted, and I whirled around to see what had riled the crew. The men had all gathered in a crowd with a bruised and bloodied Henry at the center of it all.

"What the fuck," I mumbled to myself as I made my way down to the main deck. I elbowed my way through the throng of men, pushing my way into the center. "What the hell is going on here? Take these shackles off of him immediately," I barked, silencing the men.

"He's a thief!" One man called from the crowd.

"Aye, and he tried to poison Miss Katherine!" said another.

"Poison? What are you even talking about?" My mind whirled with the ridiculous accusations. Before anyone else could answer, the men parted, and heavy foot falls announced the arrival of Teach.

"Captain, these long days at sea have addled their brains. The men are restless, and poor Henry here has become good entertainment," I explained, waving it off.

"I disagree," he said as he stroked his beard. "You, yourself, informed me of Miss Katherine's condition, did you not?"

"Well, yes, but that has nothing to do with Henry," I said, glaring at him. I could feel it in my gut. Teach was up to something.

"As it were, I found a cup of strange herbs at her bedside. Turns out, someone pilfered Cook's rations just this morning. The coincidence didn't sit well with me, so I questioned some of the men, and with a little encouragement, each of them pointed a finger at Henry."

"That's a goddamned lie, and you know it!" I challenged.

"Is it though?"

"It was on my orders that Henry took the herbs from the galley. If you're looking for someone to punish, I'm your man," I admitted. I wouldn't let Teach punish Henry just to get to me.

"Best choose your words carefully. Are you saying that it was you who tried to poison my whore?" he asked. The surrounding men hung on our every word. I could see the excitement flare in their eyes the moment the accusations pointed to me. Tensions had been building in the long months at sea. The men needed a distraction, and nothing would suit that need better than the first mate being punished for such an indiscretion. Especially when the sentence for such a crime was death.

All of them stood, silently waiting for my confession. I swallowed hard, trying to calculate my next move. Teach had me by the balls, and the smug grin on his face told me he knew it.

"It was me," Henry broke the silence.

"No, Henry, don't—"

"I did it of my own accord. James had nothing to do with my thieving, but I never tried to hurt Miss Katherine."

"Liar!" A man shouted and the crew erupted. They were bloodthirsty and wouldn't settle for anything less. I was pushed aside as the men surged toward Henry. I kept my eyes locked with his. I could see the resignation in them. He knew this was it. I was the one who was having a hard time accepting it.

Teach hadn't needed to dispense a punishment. The crew were judge, jury, and executioner. The captain only watched as they dragged him into the rigging. A lump formed in my throat. Henry was a good man. The only man I'd ever considered a friend, and he would die because of me. I stood stoic, clenching my fists at my side. My heart told me I was a coward for standing by while they murdered him. But my rational side knew that if I tried to save him, we'd both die, and his sacrifice would have been in vain.

Henry never took his eyes off me, and I forced myself to hold his gaze. The only comfort I could offer in this hopeless situation was to let him know he wasn't alone. With a cheer from the crowd, they pushed Henry from the crow's nest, swinging from the mast by his neck. His whole body twisted on the rope, struggling as his face turned purple. My stomach lurched as I watched him suffer. I could feel a part of my soul crack and shatter. My hand was on my pistol, curling around the handle too tightly. I paused momentarily, asking the Divine to save my broken soul, then I fired a shot. Henry stilled instantly, a stain of blood spreading across his chest as his limp body swayed in the wind. The men whooped with morbid glee as they made sport of throwing rotten apples at his lifeless body. As they celebrated, I felt as though I were losing my grasp on reality. The image was forever etched into my memory. His suffering was over, but mine was only growing worse.

# CHAPTER FIFTEEN
## -BROKEN-
### Katherine

I t was a gunshot. I knew that sound. It was unmistakable. I dropped the small sketch I'd been working on. The pounding of my heart drowned out the flutter of falling papers. Was it James? Did that single shot have his name on it? Edward was deteriorating the closer we got to the ruby. I only hoped he wasn't completely mad by the time we reached it.

The sound of heavy boots in the passageway had me on my feet. I stumbled toward the bed, tripping over my full skirts, desperate to retrieve the dagger hidden under my pillow. A nervous breath escaped my lips when my fingers curled around the cool handle. The footfalls grew louder as they approached my room. Either my fate or my executioner hid behind the door. Keys fumbled against the metal lock, threatening to break the fraying hold I had on the panic rising in my chest. When the door swung open, my fear evaporated.

"Oh James! Thank goodness you're alright," I breathed, dropping the dagger and clutching at my still racing heart. He lingered in the shadows of the passageway, silently staring at me.

"James?" I questioned as I took a step toward him. His brilliant blue eyes were dark, and deep lines etched his face in a scowl. The tempest within him raged out of control. A chill ran up my spine. This was a different version of the man I loved. "James, what's happened?"

"It's Henry. He's gone," he said mechanically, his words devoid of emotion. I gasped, a knot of sadness welling up in my throat. I knew what Henry meant to James, and my heart broke for him.

"What happened?" I asked, taking another hesitant step toward him, unsure of how to comfort him.

"Teach." The name rolled off his lips in a growl. "Please tell me we're close, because I'm not sure how much longer I can do this." I grabbed for his hand, pulling him into the soft light of my room, closing the door behind us. James had always been so cautious, ensuring our relationship remained hidden, but he wasn't thinking clearly. His normal discretion had been replaced by grief.

"We are close." I told him what he needed to hear. The visions didn't work in absolutes. Everything was always fluid. But the look in his eyes forced the lie. I had to give him something to hold on to. "I can't say for certain. Likely we have only a few days at the most. What can I do? Tell me how I can help you?" I took a chance and stepped into him, wrapping my arms around his neck.

He stiffened at my touch, and my heart sank.

"What is that?" he asked, a frantic tone overriding his melancholy.

"What is what?" I followed his gaze until my eyes landed on the drawing that had fallen to the floor.

"It's just a sketch." I said, taken aback by his strange comment. He stooped over, picking up the drawing pad, tracing his fingers over the lines of the apple I'd been drawing.

"Why an apple? Are you trying to torment me too?"

"I don't understand what you're talking about."

"The apple, Kat! Why are you drawing a fucking apple? Did he put you up to this?" He shouted at me, his fingers digging into my shoulders in an iron grip.

"James, you're scaring me."

"Tell me now, why were you drawing an apple?" His wild eyes were locked on mine as he waited for a response.

"I just was!" I said defensively. "I found an apple in my

room. I was trying to distract myself. Drawing helps me to forget." James let out a sigh, his grip loosened on my arms.

"I'm going mad, Kat. That man will be the death of me. The apples—I've been seeing them everywhere. Either he knows of our betrayal, or the Divine is conspiring to drive me insane."

"An apple?"

"Yes, don't you see? The ultimate forbidden fruit. It's a sign."

"He can't know. We'd both be dead if he did," I said, changing the subject from James' delusions.

"Don't look at me like that, Kat. That's what he wants. He wants to drive a wedge between us. He wants you to believe that I've lost my mind. That's why he hasn't killed us. Death would be too easy. He means to fuck with us, break us down. It's not enough for him to kill my body. He plans to kill my soul, too."

"James," I said his name softly, pushing a strand of hair back from his face. "I won't let him break us. I know you're not losing your mind. We *will* survive this. We just need to hold it together a little while longer."

"I never should have brought you on this ship. Everything that's happened is my fault."

"I would have been burning on the witch's pyre if you hadn't saved me."

"And I would have been a moth following you into the flames." He pulled me toward him, his lips finding mine in an urgent kiss. "Katherine, I don't want to wait anymore. I don't know how much time we have left. I need to lose myself inside you."

"I want you, too, but not like this. You're hurting. You're not thinking clearly. We made a vow, and if I take advantage of you now, we'll both regret it in the morning. If there is one thing in my life that I will do right, it's this."

"But what if we don't survive? I'll be doomed to an eternity in hell without ever knowing what your heaven feels like."

"This isn't the end. There is more of our story to tell. If we die on this ship, we'll find each other again in the next life. Maybe that one won't be so painful."

James sighed, his forehead resting against mine. "Why didn't anyone warn me that love is nothing more than blissful anguish?"

"And you, my love, are waxing poetic," I giggled. I could feel the tension melt out of him and his shoulders slumped as he held me close.

"What I wouldn't give to have you make me forget life for a night. Thank you for reminding me I can still be an honorable man," he sighed, the weight of so much sorrow still lingering in his voice. "I should probably go. I need to put my friend to rest. I'll be laying low as best I can for the next few days." He kissed my forehead and turned to go.

"James, look out for yourself. We have a date with destiny, and you best not keep me waiting."

IT HAD BEEN three days since Henry's death. I hadn't seen James since that night. I'd been relegated to my room. Teach reassigned the cabin boy to my care, and he was the only visitor I had. He spent as little time as possible to bring me meals and clean clothes. He'd been completely mute, ignoring the barrage of questions I asked every time he entered my room. Even Edward had been absent. In the quiet space where there was no one to save me from my own thoughts, I felt like I was losing my own grasp on reality. Maybe James was right, and he knew. I spent my days confined to the small room. Pacing what was now my prison. Even drawing didn't seem to settle my fickle mind.

The only solace I had were the random pieces of parchment slipped under my door. The romantic quotes scribbled in James' hand were the only proof that he was still alive.

*I will live in thy heart, die in thy lap, and be buried in thy eyes,*

was the quote written on his note this morning. Shakespeare's line from *Much Ado About Nothing* seemed an ominous premonition from my lover. I'd gone to the door the moment it had appeared, and called out for him. But there was nothing. I slipped my finger under the door, like we'd done so many times before, and yet they remained cold. No warm touch to give me comfort.

I flung myself on the bed, the isolation finally breaking me. Manifesting in a well of tears that wouldn't stop. I was supposed to be a strong, capable woman. At least that was the armor I hid behind. But I couldn't be strong anymore. At any moment, a kraken could swallow the ship, and I knew I was ready. I was ready to welcome the peaceful oblivion the ocean offered. Then none of this would matter. My chance at happiness rested on a knifes blade. One wrong move and I'd be gutted. Was any of this truly worth it? The suffering I'd endured just to roll the dice one time. I was beginning to realize the odds had never been in my favor.

I stayed on the bed, shamelessly crying out every sorrow from years of abuse until I had no more tears left to cry. My skin felt tight against my bones, my eyes swollen and burning, when the sound of keys scraping against the metal lock of my door announced an unexpected visitor. The door burst open, slamming against the wall. Edward stumbled in. One look at him and I knew he wasn't in his right mind. Lit cannon fuses sparked from his beard, a tactic he reserved for his enemies. His eyes rolled in his head, and he struggled to keep his balance, a bottle of rum spilling on the ground as he staggered into my room.

"There you are, whore," he said, slurring his words. I glared at him. My pride locking up any words I had for this man. I was damned no matter what I said. He grabbed a fistful of my hair, dragging me to my feet and pulling me from the room. I couldn't hold back the scream that escaped my lips as a shock of pain radiated from my head.

He pulled me up the narrow stairs and onto the main deck. It was the first time I'd breathed fresh air in days. The sun was just beginning its descent into the infinite horizon, lighting the sky in a blood orange. The beauty of it seemed unjust when my world was nothing but darkness.

"Edward! What are you doing?" I screeched. My panic rising as a hoard of men waited for me on deck with eager eyes. The setting sun cast their faces in dark shadows.

"I'm in a giving mood. These men have served me honorably. They have been the picture of loyalty..." He exaggerated the word before continuing. "I think they deserve to be rewarded. What do you say, lads?" The men all grunted their approval. Their wicked snickers crawling all over my body before they'd even touched me. They couldn't hide the excitement in their eyes. Months at sea had whittled away their morals, and now they were nothing more than feral dogs.

"Please, Edward. Please!" I begged. My pride crumbled, and I would have said anything to stop whatever he had in mind.

"Katherine, you're nothing more than property. Either, you're mine and I'll share you with my friends. Or you're not, and I'll give you a fate worse than death."

With his fingers still embedded in my hair, he pushed me over a cannon, shackling my hands around the barrel.

It took only a moment before the first man took up position behind me. I recognized his face. His name was Gunder. The new bo'sun that weaseled his way up the ranks. He took the spot when James was promoted to first mate. The stench of his unkempt body stung my nose as he pushed my skirts over my back, exposing me to the gathered crew. I'd never been a modest woman, but my cheeks heated as the sheer embarrassment of my position broke me down even further.

I could feel him, hot and hard against my leg, ready to take me without a second thought. Frantic fingers tried to force their way inside me, and all I could picture were his filthy hands and dirt-caked fingernails. Bile rose in my throat, and I struggled to hold the contents of my stomach down.

"You're dry as a bone," he grumbled in my ear. "Did Captain break ya?" He chuckled to himself as he squeezed my breast. "No matter. I'll take his sloppy seconds on the account that you're easy on the eyes." He snorted then, clearing his throat, and I heard the unmistakable sound of him spitting into his hand. I jumped when he slapped my sex. His thick sputum sliding down my leg. I couldn't be here. This wasn't my life. I squeezed my eyes closed, desperate to shut everything out. To be anywhere but here. The lewd jeers, the snide laughter, broke my focus and there was no escape.

"Kathrine!" The familiar voice flooded my mind.

I heard the scuffle of feet behind me, followed by a

hollowed groan. A warm trickle splattered against my back and then he was gone. A heavy thud rattled the planks beside me and Gunder's vacant eyes stared up at me from the deck, blood covering his chest from a gaping slit in his throat.

"Edward, call off the men and unchain her now, before I send the rest of them to hell." James' voice was deadly calm.

# CHAPTER SIXTEEN
## -LOYALTY-

### James

"Ahh, James. I was wondering how long it would take. Took you a fair bit longer than I expected. But showing your true colors, nonetheless," Teach sneered at me. My fingers flexed around the hilt of my cutlass, my knuckles turning white as I gripped it too tightly. Using every restraint I had not to attack him then and there.

The sight of their dirty hands on her— it had broken something within me. And Teach had orchestrated the whole thing to provoke me. Unraveling whatever remnants of loyalty I had for the man. I was done being his puppet. I would never again bow to anyone.

But Kat would bear the brunt of my foolishness if I completely lost my head and got myself killed.

"If you have a problem with me, then let's settle it like men. Don't be a fucking coward and use a helpless woman to get at me."

"This was a test of loyalty, and you both failed miserably. My first mate, helping himself to my property behind my back," he tsked, shaking his head in a dramatic display of disappointment. "If I can't trust you with my whore, than there is no hope for you."

"If you'd grant me an audience to explain. I think I've earned at least that much."

"You'll have plenty of time, and I promise you'll spill every sordid detail of your betrayal. That is what you've earned, boy!"

"I won't make it easy on you," I challenged, pulling a dagger into my free hand, ready to pay whatever the cost. I wouldn't hide my love for Kat in the shadows any longer.

"I hadn't expected you to, but we have you considerably outnumbered. Don't we, lads?" The men shouted approval, eager to exact whatever revenge they felt they were owed.

"Aye, but I know I have fate on my side. Katherine's told me as much." I could see a flash of fear in his eyes. The possibility that my words held even a grain of truth, were eating away at him.

"Take him down alive, but make sure he suffers for his

treason against us." Teach stepped back, lighting a cigar from the burning cannon fuse at his beard, the cherry red ember flaring as he sat back to watch my demise.

I stood, protectively in front of Kat. I wouldn't let any of them touch her.

"Which one of you wants to be the next one down?" I taunted. These men knew me. I was counting that as one of the few assets I had. The reputation I'd earned would make them second guess their actions, giving me the upper hand in these unfavorable odds. No one answered. No one moved. There was utter silence. Even the sea, in its unnatural calmness, was quietly waiting for the inevitable chaos.

As if some unseen signal had been given, they burst into action, coming at me two at a time. All of them cowards. Afraid to face me man to man. I tried to stay by Kat's side, but with every step of the lethal dance, I was pulled further and further away. The deafening silence was now filled with the clashing of steel against steel. My cutlass unapologetically releasing them of their last breath added an unmistakably haunting wail to the battle cries piercing the night air.

I relied on my years of training to guide me. Drawing out the brutal killer that Teach had created. I put every ounce of energy I had into this final stand. I was holding my own until I caught sight of Teach in my periphery. He was heading straight for Katherine.

"Don't you fucking touch her!" I screamed, but my words were lost in the chaos. I continued to swing my sword, my eyes darting between Kat and my attackers. Teach had her in his grasp. Her pleading screams ripped at my soul. I couldn't get to her. He was dragging her away from me. "Teach! Teach, you fucking bastard! I will kill you!"

Anger boiled over as they disappeared below deck. I surged forward, but there were too many. The onslaught of rage blinded me in a dance where there was no room for error. A well placed elbow caught my ribs, forcing the air from my lungs. I stumbled backward, losing my dagger. It was my first misstep, and they made me pay for it. A noose was slipped around my neck from behind. Tightening until I could barely pull in a breath. Leashing me like a stray dog, they restrained my arms. The cowards took turns landing blow after blow on my gut. Blackness bled into my vision, threatening to consume me. I refused to give up—not with Katherine in his grasp.

The ground shifted violently under my feet, and the ship lurched starboard, sending all of us sprawling across the deck. Reaching for the noose around my neck, I pulled it slack and sucked in a much needed breath. Getting back to Kat was the only thing I focused on. The wind began to pick up, catching the sails and tossing the ship back to port. A dizzying nausea washed over me before I managed to get to my feet. The crew shifted from bloodlust to wide eyed concern in a matter of mere moments.

Thunder-less lightning skittered across the sky, momentarily highlighting a sea that was beginning to churn underneath us. A shudder traveled from stern to bow. The planks groaned in protest.

"Whatcha think it is?" One of the men asked.

"Probably just a whale rubbing against the keel," another answered.

"Mister James, what would you have us do?" The swabbie asked as the groans grew louder. I laughed to myself for a moment. The spell had been broken. Their sinister intent instantly dissolved the moment a new threat presented itself.

"I'm not the first mate of the *Queen Anne* any longer. You're on your own."

A scream pierced the night air, and we all stared in disbelief. The cabin boy's body hung above the deck. A massive tentacle wrapped around his chest. He lingered in mid air only for a moment before it recoiled back into the sea, dragging the screaming man into the depths with it. Another loud crack from the hull sent the crew scurrying. With Teach still absent and the bo'sun dead, there was no one to take charge. They devolved into a hoard of ants, mindlessly running in all directions. I was entranced by the sight. My feet pinned to the deck, the demon in my chest purred as the kraken began to offer up sweet revenge.

The man beside me was ripped off his feet, a burnt orange tentacle enveloped him from his chest to his thigh. "Help me! Please!" he begged. His hands stretched out to me. Fear clouding his eyes as the kraken carried him off to his death. A normal man would have been spurred into action, but any empathy I had died a long time ago. Now I only smiled at the sight. They'd all earned this, and nothing could please me more than watching them get what they deserved.

Waves crashed over the bow as the *Queen Anne* floundered. The roar of cannons and the screams of men were drown out by the raging storm. The scent of black powder carried on the whipping winds, and I stood like a crazed man at the center of it all, reveling in the spectacle.

Large tentacles slammed onto the deck. The monster of the deep hauled it's massive body up until one inky black eye was staring at me. The creature grumbled and let out a shriek like I'd never heard. My hands covered my ears, but it wasn't enough. The sound brought me to my knees, and it felt as though my head might split in half. It wasn't until the beasts keening subsided that I was reminded that I wasn't simply a spectator. The ship was heavily favoring her starboard side. The *Queen Anne* was on her last breath, and I had to get to Kat. I catapulted into action, getting below deck only to find a flood of water rushing in around my ankles. I was tossed about the hallways as I waded through the rising water. We were running out of time.

"Kat! Kat! Where are you!"

"Here! I'm here!" Her muffled voice called. She was in the captain's quarters.

I barreled down the passageway, colliding with the door. The rushing water making it almost impossible to wedge it open.

"James, please hurry! We're sinking. You have to get me out!" My eyes settled on Kat's panicked face. The water was up to her waist, and she was chained to Teach's bed. No sign of the captain anywhere. "He left the keys just out of my reach." The sick fuck had placed the keys just far enough for her to see her freedom, but not close enough to ever grasp it.

"I've got you. Don't worry, we're getting out of here. This is what we wanted." I tried to sound calm and reassuring while I retrieved the keys, but the water was rising alarmingly fast. Eerie groans filled the cabin, an ominous reminder that at any moment the ship could be torn apart. We were on borrowed time. Adrenaline roared in my veins, urging me to move faster, but I couldn't stop my hands from fumbling with the keys.

The water reached our chests by the time I got the shackles off her. The heavy Victorian dress she wore slowed her down, but there was no time to cut it off. I gripped her hand in mine, determined never to let it go. We lived or we died together.

The flooded passageway was now completely tilted on its side, our heads just barely bobbing above the water.

"James. I want you to know that I'll love you even into the shadows of the next life," she said, and it sounded like a goodbye.

"Don't do that. We're going to make it out of here," I commanded, not allowing any other thoughts to enter my mind.

The *Queen Anne* was sinking on her port side when we crawled our way to the deck. I had prepared to escape with Kat on a dinghy when the kraken finally struck, but it had all happened too late. Teach had foiled our plans. Now I was desperate for a way out.

Before a plan could even take shape in my head, a resounding crack echoed in my ears and my body was airborne, flung from the ship. I couldn't tell which way was up or down. The only solid was Kat's hand in mine. We hit the water hard, forcing the air from my lungs and knocking me senseless. I could tell that we were sinking, but I couldn't bring myself to care. I couldn't summon the strength to move.

The demon burned in my chest, forcing my eyes to pop open. The sea held us in its weightless embrace. Moonlight filtered into the dark water, illuminating Kat's face. Her eyes were closed. Peaceful. Her golden hair swirled around her face, and she looked like a beautiful specter. But she wasn't dead. She was vibrant and filled with life, but if I did nothing, we were both lost souls. It was the thought of her body, dead and rotting at the bottom of the sea that spurred me into action. The urge to live reigniting inside me. I wrapped an arm around her and kicked. Everything inside me ached and burned, but I kept going. The peaceful embrace of the sea quickly turned into death's stranglehold. My vision clouded, but my resolve was steadfast.

When I finally broke the surface, that first breath felt like a renewal. I'd done so many things wrong in my life, but fate had given Kat and I a second chance. I wouldn't fuck it up this time. *Queen Anne's Revenge* was nothing more than splintered driftwood. Most of the ship was making its slow descent into the depths, but broken pieces of the hull still remained afloat. I managed to pull Katherine to a section of the ship and haul her waterlogged body aboard. She still hadn't moved. Hadn't pulled in a breath. I crawled onto the wreckage with her lifeless body.

"Katherine! Wake up!" I patted her cheeks and shook her shoulders, but she didn't move. Panic began to rise in my chest. Was I too late? Had I lingered in purgatory for too long? Had she gone on without me?

Frantically, I pushed down on her chest. Willing her to take a breath. I kept pushing, I wouldn't give up. That's not how she'd said it would happen.

"Breathe, goddamn you! I won't let you leave me. Not now." Water poured from her mouth and her whole body convulsed as she expelled the sea water. I turned her on her side, her body heaving with raking coughs. The sound was like music to my ears.

"James," she rasped, flopping over on her back, trying to catch her breath. "Did we make it?"

"Yes, we made it." I smiled down at her, riding on the high of simply being alive. The storm had passed, and the seas were quiet again. No evidence that anyone had survived the kraken's wrath, save for the two of us. Kat stared up at the night sky as we floated away from the devastation.

"The stars. I've seen this pattern before, over and over again, just how they are placed in the sky now." She sat up, hope flaring in her eyes. "This is it. This is the path we were meant to be on."

# CHAPTER SEVENTEEN
## -MINE-

### James

The gentle bob of the ocean waters roused me from my dreamless sleep. The sun had yet to rise above the horizon, but the stars were already lost in her light. It was eerily silent. Nothing but the lapping water against the broken piece of hull. The only remains of the chaos we had endured. No more screams, no more cannon blasts, no more splintering wood. Not even a bird flying above. The *Queen Anne's Revenge* and her crew were simply gone. Nothing left but a memory of the horrors she possessed. We'd barely escaped the kraken last night. That monstrous creature would haunt the darkest corners of my mind til my dying days. I took a moment and thanked the Divine for their mercy.

I'd spent the evening kicking towards the shoreline. The sheer fear of the kraken grabbing ahold of my ankle, like one of Neverland's mermaids, kept me moving into the wee hours of morning. When my legs refused to go any further, I climbed atop of our makeshift raft, pulled Kat into my arms, and fell victim to exhaustion. The current had worked in our favor, pushing us closer to our salvation while we slept. The island was just ahead.

"Kat, my love." I gently nudged her. "Wake up, we made it." I placed a kiss on her forehead as she opened her eyes.

"We're alive?" she mumbled.

"Alive and at the doorstep of our future." I pushed an errant strand of hair from her face and kissed her soft lips. "We did it. Look."

She sat up, quickly taking in our surroundings. It was just us and the island. "We're free," she giggled at the realization. "We're free!"

I pulled her into an embrace, effectively tipping our raft over and sending us splashing into waist deep water. Laughing, I lifted Kat into my arms and kissed her fiercely. I claimed her mouth, tasting the salt of the sea, knowing that Manann had bestowed us with his blessing. "Come, let us find our ruby." Grabbing her hand, we walked together toward the shoreline.

The island was beautifully alluring. If I learned anything

from my time in Neverland, it was that beautiful things were not always what they seemed. This was the hiding spot of a powerful relic. We would be wise to be mindful. Craggy peaks rose up from the center, attempting to kiss the clouds. While white sugar sand beaches littered the rocky shoreline. Small palm trees and bushes shrouded the dense landscape, effectively hiding the secrets within. We had no map to guide us. Just my intuition and Kat's visions.

"This place is paradise." Kat was in awe. "Are you sure you don't want to just stay here for eternity? Our own little oasis." She started looking around the private beach. "We could build a little hut here and live off the land."

"Be wary, my love. Often, beauty is but a dangerous illusion. We should try to find the ruby quickly and make our way back to Neverland. Who knows what this island is hiding."

"Fear not, James," she said theatrically. "For we have escaped hell and have found our heaven." A coy smile spread across her face as she closed the distance between us, reaching up on her tiptoes to pull me to her sinful mouth. I slid my hands into her wet hair, pulling her closer, tilting her head to deepen the kiss. Her soft lips parted eagerly, and my tongue swept over hers. The delicate kiss escalated to a fevered pitch. I explored every curve of her mouth in a wild abandon. She kissed me back with a fervor of her own, dragging her teeth over my bottom lip.

Greedy with need, she ripped at my soggy shirt. "I want you now," she demanded. "We have waited long enough. We have fulfilled our vow. I will not wait any longer." Her hands roamed my body, dropping lower to my growing length. This was it. The moment I had been so desperately waiting for.

I growled at the heat of her touch. "Slow down, love. We've waited years for this moment. There is no need to rush. He can't hurt us anymore." I pulled my shirt over my head. Her chilled fingers slid slowly down my damp chest, sending a shiver of pleasure down my spine. I turned her gently away from me and began pulling at laces of her dress. One by one, I took my time freeing her from the soaked gown. I wanted to savor every moment. I was determined to do this right and worship the perfection of her body that had been denied to me for so long. I slipped the gown off her shoulders and dropped it in a heap at her sandy feet. I spun her back towards me and lifted the wet shift from her body. Her skin pebbled with the cool breeze, begging to be soothed by my touch.

"Your beauty..." I paused, searching for the right words. "It leaves me utterly speechless," I admitted as my hungry eyes drank in the sight of her. She was the reason I made it this far without the demon swallowing me whole. The one thing that could dull the aching need for revenge, at least for a short while anyway. I lifted her chin and kissed her gently before scooping her up in my arms, and laying her down on the soft, warm sand.

"Touch me," she mewed.

Her back arched as my hand caressed her perfect breasts.

She groaned as I rolled her nipple between my thumb and forefinger, gently squeezing. I dipped my head down, pulling her nipple into my mouth. I teased her sensitive flesh with my tongue before pinching it with my teeth, eliciting a guttural moan. She liked the pain, and it excited me even more. My cock begged for release. The careful control I had on the raw hunger was slipping, but I wasn't done playing with her yet. My pleasure would come once she'd had hers.

I kissed my way down her soft belly, pressing her thighs back, exposing her beautiful sex. She was slick with desire, practically writhing with need. I slowly dragged my tongue along her wetness. I tasted her sweet excitement and realized I'd been a starved man. Her hands gripped my hair and pressed my face deeper into her core. I was awash in her desire and surrounded by her scent. I began to tease her clit, drawing out cries of pleasure. I was completely under her spell, lost in her ecstasy.

I massaged her opening with two fingers, gently stretching her before sliding them deep inside her.

"James," she cried out as pleasure consumed her. Hearing her say my name while she writhed beneath me was something I'd never tire of.

"That's my good girl," I purred as her sex clamped around my fingers.

"More," she begged. I obliged, sliding in yet another finger, my tongue circling her swollen clit. "Yes," she groaned as her thighs pulled in, locking around my head. She bucked her hips, lost in the throes of orgasm, riding out the sensation on my fingers. Her pleasure only fanned my desire. I needed to be inside her, now. I ripped open my breeches and freed my cock from its prison.

Sliding the head of my length through her wetness, coating myself in her warm release. I aligned myself at her entrance, teasing her with just the tip, circling the tender skin.

"James, please," she begged. "Take me now."

Her words drove my need to the brink of desperation. I buried myself to the hilt in one deep thrust, groaning with my own pleasure. We fit together perfectly. She was warm and tight—everything I had ever imagined. She was made for me. I reveled in the rawness of the moment. Her emerald eyes peered up at me, naked with emotion from the years that had been stolen from us, but time be damned, now she was truly mine.

Slowly, I began to thrust in and out. I had waited so long for this moment that I couldn't control myself. My pace quickened, and Katherine cried out, begging for more. My thrusting became pounding as I lost all control of my body. Our breathing became ragged, my movements animalistic as I ground my hips into hers. I pulled her leg up, angling so I could take her deeper. The sound of her pleasure, the feel of her warmth around me, pushed me to the precipice until together we fell into momentary delirium. Her sex gripped my cock, milking every ounce of desire I had built up over the years. I collapsed on top of her, breathless. Our breathing synchronized in the aftermath of our bliss.

"I love you, Miss Katherine Hawkins," I whispered into her ear.

"I love you too, Mr. James." She smiled as I kissed her forehead.

"I would have waited lifetimes for that moment." I'd never known such pleasure, such love. To be truly desired by a woman. I wanted to stay in this moment forever, never having to fear being without her again. I allowed us to be indulgent for a moment while we enjoyed each other's embrace, but we couldn't linger here for long. The island gave me pause, and I didn't trust it to be the paradise it portrayed. There were secrets hidden here.

"I would love nothing more than to spend the day worshiping your divine body, but I do not trust this island. I don't think we should stay in one place for too long. We should start searching for the ruby. We don't want to lose daylight."

"James, relax. The sun has just now shown us his face. We have the entire day. Can't we spend some time exploring each other?" Her words were thick with lust and threatened to pull me from my endeavors.

"Katherine, I promise you, once we are in Neverland, I will spend my days bringing you endless pleasure." I stood up, pulling my breeches back on. "We need to keep moving. It's not safe here."

She sighed, clearly annoyed with my need to move. "Once we make it to Neverland, I'll hold you to that promise."

I chuckled at her mocking response. "I promise you'll be begging for reprieve."

Smirking at me, she began to pull on her damp clothes.

"Leave your wet dress behind. It will only hinder your movement. Besides if you only wear your shift, I can stare at your perfect breasts." I waggled my eyebrows at her suggestively. "Now, what exactly did you see in your vision with Manann?"

"The ruby is in a dark place, somewhere hidden from the sun. A cave maybe?"

"Perfect! There is a peak at the center of the island. Let's go find us a cave."

THE ISLAND FOREST was thick with shrubs and sprawling vines, making it difficult to trek through. With each swing of my cutlass, I imagined cleaving Pan. Hacking off his limbs, one by one, in blood soaked bedlam. We were so close I could taste it. The ruby was with in reach. Revenge would be mine.

"James! Look! Through the vines, is that an opening in the mountainside?"

My pace quickened. Just ahead, along the sheer wall of rock, hiding behind the dense vines, was indeed an opening. Excitement took over as I hacked away at the vegetation. It was small, just large enough to crawl through, and covered with spider webs. It appeared to open up at the end. More of a chute than an actual cave. "It looks like there's water down there. I can see light reflecting off the surface." I tossed a pebble and listened for the splash. It wasn't a long drop. I had routinely taken worse in Neverland just to get to the mermaid lagoon.

"This has to be it. I can feel power surging here." Kat began to wring her hands and pace back and forth.

"I'm going in. You wait here until I tell you it's safe."

"I don't like this, James. What if it's a trap? How will we get you out?"

"It's a risk I'm willing to take... for us." I would risk it all to get back to Pan. Having Katherine by my side shone a light in the darkness. But the hard truth was, if she had chosen not to come back with me, I would have carried on without her. It would have broken my heart, ripped a hole in my soul, but I would have gone on without her. There was no choice. Nothing would stop me. I was going in.

"Be careful. I'm not ready to say goodbye to you yet. We just—"

I leaned down, interrupting her worrisome thoughts and kissed her as though it were the last time. Memorizing the feel of her soft, full lips against mine. Breathing in her intoxicating scent. "The Divine has brought us this far. I trust in our destiny." I hugged her tightly before I sat on the ground, sliding my legs through the hole. I turned to look at Kat one last time and whispered the words, "I love you," before dropping down into the dark unknown.

With a thud, I landed on a small rocky ledge at the edge of the water. Golden light shone from somewhere up ahead, illuminating the beautiful cerulean water. Roots dropped from the mossy ceiling, dangling like the disfigured fingers of some evil woodland fae. Reaching down, I tapped the water's edge in an attempt to summon some unknown foe or trigger some chain reaction.

There were no signs of life other than the island flora. It was silent, but for the familiar sound of running water off in the distance. There was a waterfall somewhere in this cavern. I was sure of it.

"Kat! All's well. Come down. I'll catch you." Without hesitation, she slid down the chute. "I've got you." I reached up, gripping her calfs and helped her down to the ground.

"What is this place?"

"I'm not sure, but we are going to find out. Keep your eyes and ears open."

The water was knee deep and quickly grew deeper as we made our way toward the beaming light. The opening up ahead appeared to be massive. All we could see on the other side of the tunnel were the same rocky moss-covered walls.

"James," Katherine called my name. Unease trembled in her voice. She had stopped moving, completely frozen in fear. "I'm having a hard time keeping my feet grounded. The pull from the water is too strong." She was submerged up to her chest and a strong current was forming as we neared what appeared to be the edge of the opening. The sound of rushing water grew louder with each step and my suspicions were becoming reality.

"I think we're coming up on a waterfall. Kat, I need you to brace yourself. I'm coming. We are going to go slow and steady. One step at a time." I reached out my hand to grab her, grazing her fingertips as she was pulled off her feet. "Kat!" I screamed her name, desperately trying to reach her, watching in horror as the water pulled her under.

Gasping for air, she bobbed up several feet away from me. "Kat!" I screamed her name again before she disappeared under the water. In an act of desperation, I pulled in a deep breath and lifted my feet from the ground, allowing the current to pull me under, toward my beloved. I tried to swim with the flowing current, but before I could gather my bearings, I felt myself being thrown off the lip of the tunnel, plummeting down in a punishing rush of water. I tried to surface, but the water kept pummeling me back down, tossing me around like a piece of seaweed caught in the tide. I didn't know up from down. My lungs began to burn with need. Panic consumed my mind. This couldn't be the end. I kicked hard against the barrage of pelting water. My boot hit something hard. It had to be the bottom of the cavern. I pushed with all my might and finally found a break in the onslaught. I bobbed up to the surface and gasped for air.

"Kat!" I cried out. Frantically, I started searching the cavern for any sign of her. "Katherine!" Light shone through in bars from above, illuminating the massive cavern. The waterfall had dropped us hundreds of feet. She should have surfaced by now. My heart began to pound in my chest. Anxiety consumed my thoughts. Katherine was gone.

# CHAPTER EIGHTEEN
## -ULTIMATUM-

### *James*

The roar of water cascading over the sheer cliff was deafening, adding to the chaos in my mind. I couldn't think clearly. Katherine was nowhere to be found.

"Kat! Where are you?" I screamed, but it was no use. I sunk below the water, searching the darkness for any sign of life. A shimmer of blonde hair caught my eye, light glinting on the golden strands as they drifted deeper into the water. The flash of a colorful fin was the last thing I saw before she disappeared under the rocks.

I surfaced for a moment, sucking in a lungful of air, and

pulled a dagger from my belt before diving under again. I pushed myself hard. My abused body protesting as I propelled myself deeper. It was as if I could hear her voice echoing in the surrounding water. Calling my name. Luring me down. I reached the spot where I'd lost track of her, only to find an opening in the cavern wall. A faint shimmer of light filtered down the passageway. I swore I could see the gauzy fabric of a shift around pale legs before the sight of her vanished again. I didn't hesitate. Grabbing the confining rock walls, I pulled myself through the tunnel. The rocks tore at my fingers, my blood swirling in the tides as I pulled myself along. My lungs burned in protest from the lack of air, but I was beginning to get accustomed to the sensation of drowning and I simply ignored it. There was no turning back now.

The rock walls fell away, opening into a large lagoon. Breaking the surface, I gasped, desperate to catch my breath. My feet found solid ground, and I instinctively drew into a defensive pose. My dagger poised and ready. I swiped at my eyes, trying to clear the salt water. Before I could focus, the sound of their laughter sent a shiver down my spine. Like the sweet peel of bells echoing off the cavernous walls. I knew that sickly sweet sound anywhere. It was the sirens of the deep—mermaids.

I hadn't seen a mermaid since I left Neverland's shores. And an urgent warning buzzed in my ear. Beautiful things aren't always what they seem. Mermaids were the perfect example of this. My eyes caught on bright orange hair hanging in waves around a familiar, preternaturally beautiful face. It was Elordis, Queen Mother of the mermaids. My jaw fell open at the sight of her. It couldn't be her. Mermaids didn't exist in this realm, and yet here she was. I knew I wasn't mistaken. I'd tussled with her a time or two back in Neverland. She'd been *in* Neverland. The fact that she was here now, in this realm, was more than disturbing. But what petrified me the most was the sight of her long, pale fingers wrapped around Kat's neck.

"See, sisters, I told you. All we needed was the proper bait," Elordis teased. She had propped herself on a stack of what appeared to be human skulls. A wide-eyed Kat lay completely immobilized in her clutches. Two other mermaids circled in the water before her.

"Now that you have me here. What is it you want?" I asked, trying to engage them and buy us some time. I shifted my gaze, assessing our surroundings. My brain automatically calculating that I had a limited chance of success. The deeper we went into the belly of the mountain, the larger the caves became. This was the largest yet. Shafts of light still managed to find a way in, illuminating the rippling pools below. The turquoise waters were crystal clear and did nothing to hide the dangers of this place. The craggy bottom was littered with stark white bones. Light glinted off gold coins and steel swords. Neither had been useful in saving the men that lay in a watery grave beneath us.

"We don't get handsome visitors very often. So naturally, we wanted you to come and play with us," she cooed. Her silken sweet voice capturing my attention and breaking down my defenses.

"I'm happy to play. If you let the lady go first, I'm all yours." My eyes flicked to Kat's, silently trying to reassure her that everything was alright, even if I couldn't see a way out of this yet.

"Oh, but she's part of the fun. We need to have a toy to play with now, don't we?" She taunted, pulling a dagger from a belt around her arm. Kat whimpered as Elordis dragged the blade up her body, slicing through her shift, allowing the thin fabric to fall away from her heaving breasts.

"If you break my toy, I'll make you pay for it with your life. I don't share anymore." I snarled at her, doing my best to play along with her little game. Her two companions hissed at me as I took a step toward them.

Elordis broke into laughter once again. "I do so love it when they know how to play. I was getting a bit worried now that you've grown up."

"He broke Pan's rules. He's no longer a lost boy… but he is definitely a lost man." The blue haired one stared at me like a hungry wolf.

The mention of Peter and the Lost Boys rattled my senses. Their thrall on me loosening as the demon flexed in my chest.

"He isn't far from being a lost soul. I can see the darkness. A leech that is never satisfied. It will consume you," a third mermaid said, her flowing purple hair fanning out in the water as she circled me like prey.

I laughed maniacally. "You're a bit late. The demon has already consumed me. I am nothing more than vengeance's eager servant."

"Let us help you forget," the purple-haired one said. Her amber eyes locked on mine as she reached for me, appearing to pull a black pearl from behind my ear.

"And what if I don't want to forget?"

"While you toil in the past, Peter Pan's memories fade. You are but a mere whisper buried in his infantile mind. Stay here with us and all the horrible memories will be washed away on the tides." As she said it, the black pearl in her fingers disintegrated into a swirl of dust before it disappeared into the ether.

"I will never forget what he did. I will have what's owed to me, and no one will keep me from my prize."

"If you don't take our offer now. It will cost you everything." Elordis gave me an ultimatum. I wanted to say no. I wanted to turn her down, but the pull of their magic on my psyche was hard to resist.

"She has quite lovely breasts," she mused while I struggled to refuse their offer. "I could cut them off and you could keep them as a trophy," she offered, drawing her knife under Katherine's breast. She screamed as blood spilled over her belly, breaking through the last remnants of fog from my mind. I lunged for her, the other mermaids ensnaring my arms, holding me in place.

"Let her go! This game is over. I'm done with you."

"For a man willing to give up everything for Peter Pan,

you seem a little too attached. Let us help you." She smiled smugly and then her dagger swung in an arc, sinking the blade into Katherine's chest.

"No!" I screamed, my heart shattering as blood poured from her mouth and her eyes fluttered closed. My world shifted.

This wasn't how it was supposed to end. It had all happened so fast. Everything we had planned was gone in an instant. Revenge gave my life meaning, but Katherine... she made it all worth it. The future I'd dreamed about had slipped through my fingers as the life left her.

I was in shock. I closed my eyes, but the sight of her lifeless body was burned into my mind. I knew I should leave this place, but I couldn't bring myself to move. A part of me wanted to give in. To let them put me out of my misery and follow Kat into an afterlife that would surely be better than this, but the demon within me refused to let that happen. A burning ember of vengeance was seared into my soul. I didn't have the luxury of dying along with her. I was meant to have my revenge against Peter Pan. Fate demanded it.

The demon roared in my ears, warning me to move, but heartache overshadowed the urge to fight. It weighed on me like an anchor, pulling me down into the depths of despair. Haunting me with the specters of what might have been. Cold hands tried to drag me down, but I didn't care. I refused to open my eyes and see her dead body one more time.

*Click!*

"Get your slimy hands off of him!" The voice pulled me up short. It was her. It was Kat's voice! My eyes popped open, turning to the sound. Standing on an outcropping not a hundred yards away was Katherine. She stood with a pistol in each hand and a deep scowl on her face.

"Katherine? How is that possible?" I breathed, my heart skipping to an unnatural rhythm in my chest at the sight of her. Had I finally lost my mind? What in the name of the Divine was happening? How could she be there if she was...

Laughter filled the cave, interrupting my mental breakdown, and my eyes darted back to the mermaids. Elordis rocked with laughter, her arms no longer holding Kat's desecrated body. In its place was a barnacle crusted skeleton. Her dagger still stuck into its breast bone.

It had all been a trick. An illusion to break me down. They'd been toying with their prey.

"We were only trying to kill you," she tsked. "The man who couldn't stay a boy doesn't like our games anymore," she mocked.

The demon inside me snapped.

I lunged for her, ripping my arms free from the other two. I heard shots fired behind me, but all I could think about was wrapping my fingers around that cold, clammy skin and choking the life from her pretty little body. She pushed the skeleton from her lap, sending it toppling down the mountain of skulls she'd perched herself on. I stumbled over the old bones, temporarily distracted from my prize. I caught sight of her colorful tail disappearing on the other side of the mound. I pursued her, bones crunching under my feet. I lost my footing at the top, stumbling forward and rolling down the backside, skulls falling all around me.

"James!" I could hear Kat calling after me.

"Kat, stay here! I'll come back for you," I barked. I couldn't let the mermaid go. Not after what she'd done. Visions of Katherine's dead body would haunt me for the rest of my life.

A crack in the rock wall was the only exit point I could see. I jumped back into the water, side stepping through the crevice in the rock. Roots crisscrossed in front of me, blocking my path. My dagger swung violently as I pushed my way through the tight space. The crevice snuffed out the light plunging me into total darkness. An unnatural breeze began to pick up the further I got. The wind blew through the rocks with an ominous groan. A warning to turn back, but I pushed on. The walls seemed to tighten around me until I felt wedged into the mountain. Either I would make it through or be suffocated by the stones. I sucked in a breath, pushing further as roots pulled at my hair, scraping across my face, and blocking my view. One last push, and I was through. I was spit out into an enormous cavern. Walls soaring overhead with pinpoints of light filtering in from above, like stars casting the cave into an artificial twilight. There, swaying gently with the soft winds, was an immense three-masted ship.

# CHAPTER NINETEEN
## -DECEIT-
### James

"She's magnificent," I breathed, in awe of the ship. The sight of it had completely derailed my pursuit. There was no sign of the orange-haired mermaid. She'd vanished into the mysterious depths. My mind sifted through questions. What was this place? What secrets did it hide? And how had a ship come to rest in the belly of a mountain?

"James!" Kat's voice echoed through the narrow crevice.

"Here! I'm here!" I called back to her. Her beautiful face emerging from the darkness. A crease in her brow relaxed when she saw me, and my heart stuttered at the sight of her.

"Are you alright? What happened to the mermaid? I can't believe we made it!" Her voice shook with emotion, the words pouring out of her in a nervous rant. She wrapped her arms around me, burying her face in my neck. Her whole body trembled, and I pulled her in tighter.

"You don't have to worry about me. I'm fine. What about you?"

"I'm good. At least, I think I am. After I surfaced, I couldn't find you. Then I saw you disappearing under the water. I tried to call to you, but you couldn't hear me. What happened?"

I pulled her away from me so I could look at her. I ran my fingers over her full lips. The feel of her, real and solid and alive, soothed my soul.

"It doesn't matter. All that matters is that you're here now. Look," I said, pointing toward the massive ship.

"How... how is that possible? How did it get down here?"

"I haven't the slightest idea."

"Then there must be another way out. I don't think we can go back the way we came," she said, staring back at the dark crack we'd just come through.

I scanned the impressive cavern. There didn't appear to be another exit, at least nothing that was blatantly obvious. Definitely nothing large enough for a ship to sail through. "I don't know about you, but I'm ready to get out of the water. Are you able to swim to the ship? We can go about making a new plan once we're dry and had a moment to rest."

"Are you sure it's safe? Where did the mermaids go?"

"I followed one through here, but I don't see any sign of her now. I think the sooner we get out of the water, the better the odds are that we may live to see another dawn."

We made the short swim to the ship, and I breathed a sigh of relief that we'd been unmolested by mermaids or any number of fae that might be guarding this place. We clawed our way up the anchor chain. Our drenched bodies spilling out on the main deck. The feel of solid wooden planks beneath me was heavenly.

"Do you think we're alone here?" Kat whispered.

"Not like we were stealthy when we boarded. It looks abandoned to me," I said, trying to ease her worry. "But from what I saw back there, you can handle yourself in a fight. Where'd you even get those pistols?" I asked, a smile tugging at my lips as I propped myself on my elbow to look down at her.

"The caves are littered with gold and weapons... and a lot of dead men. Apparently, men have come here armed to the teeth, but never walked out alive."

"Then I guess it's a good thing I came with a woman. I think I need to get you a set of pistols when we get out of here. You look positively delicious when you're armed." I leaned down, brushing my lips against hers. My cock twitched in my pants. Adrenaline still pumped in my veins and the feel of her underneath me was all the encouragement I needed. I ground my hips against her, and she let out a soft moan.

"James, we should probably have a look around, don't you

think? We wouldn't want to get caught with our pants down. Plus, I need a moment to clean up."

I groaned and rested my forehead against hers. She was right, but the desire to sink myself inside her was hard to rein in when she was this close. I wrenched myself away, pulling her with me as I got to my feet.

"Come on then. Once I'm certain I have you all to myself, we can pick up where we left off."

We explored every level, searching the decks for any signs of life. The ship itself, although built in the same style as the *Queen Anne*, exhibited subtle signs that it hadn't originated from this realm. The sheer size of it alone was impressive, but we managed to clear every level. It was completely abandoned. We entered the storeroom, and it was dripping in treasure. Chests overflowed with rare jewels and gold coins marked with symbols I'd never seen in the known world. Pottery and silver sat in piles, while textiles and fine clothing overflowed the storage trunks. The fabric and design of the outfits were like the fae clothing that Teach had kept on the *Queen Anne*.

"Do you think the ruby is in here?" Kat asked.

"Possibly, but if it's as special as Teach seemed to think, I doubt it would be lumped in with the rest of the treasure. We'll have time to look for the ruby later. Why don't you find yourself something to change into, and I'll find us a place to get some sleep tonight."

She smiled at me, looking relieved to have a moment of normalcy in these wild circumstances.

"Okay. Maybe we could even find some food that hasn't spoiled in the galley."

"I already know what I'll be feasting on tonight," I growled, pulling her into me for a punishing kiss. "Come find me in the captain's quarters when you're done. And don't be long, because I'm famished."

I LEFT Katherine in the storeroom, knee deep in satin gowns. I made my way to the captain's quarters, allowing my mind to fantasize about what I could do with this ship. How it would aid me in my plans to return to Neverland eluded me at the moment, but fate had brought me here for a reason. I opened the door, finding a shadowed cabin appointed in dark mahogany. Muted light filtered in from an expansive window. From what I could see, it was spacious and neatly appointed in dark crimson fabrics. A large four poster bed was nestled to one side, and an ornate table sat at the center of the room.

I walked in and a strange sense of belonging washed over me. A feeling like coming home after so many years. Strange maps and scrolls covered the table, charting lands and seas that I had never seen before. I slid the lid from a carved box on the table and the aroma of tobacco wafted up. Cigars neatly lined the bottom, and nestled on top was an unusual contraption. I wrapped my fingers around the cold silver piece, realizing it was meant to hold two cigars to smoke at once. I helped myself, fitting two cigars into the holder and lighting a match. I pulled in a deep inhale, the tingle of tobacco lingering in my mouth before I blew out a large plume into the darkness. A creak of the floorboards was the only warning I had before a familiar face emerged from the shadows, shrouded in the swirling smoke.

"Teach," I snarled.

"Why, James, is that any way to greet your captain?" Teach said condescendingly.

"You're not my captain anymore."

"That brand on your arm says otherwise. Or have you forgotten the oath you pledged to me?"

"The moment you tried to have me killed is the moment my oath to you was broken."

"Had you not earned it? You and that little whore thought you could outsmart me? That you could be rid of me so easily? You should have cut that mark out of your arm before you deceived me."

"She is not a whore. Don't you ever fucking speak of her again!" I barked.

"You mean my property? My property that you fucked behind my back," he said, a wild look in his eyes as he took a step toward me. "Let me tell you something, boy, it'll take more than a kraken to keep me from what's mine!" He banged his fist on the table, the box of cigars spilling on the floor.

"You brought this on yourself, Teach. All those years you promised me revenge, and yet you delivered me nothing. You were a waste of my years."

"I'm to blame? I brought you under my wing when you were nothing more than a sorry excuse for a man. I taught you everything you know. How to fight. How to think. How to endure. I taught you how to be a man. I treated you like a son. I favored you over all others. We could have been unstoppable together. I warned you never to get attached, but I see now that fine pussy was your downfall." He walked around the table, glaring at me as his words set in. It wasn't a lie. He'd molded me into a ruthless killer. Only Katherine had saved me from losing my soul completely.

He chuckled then, the sound of it sending a shiver down my spine. "I guess you're right. I did bring this on myself. I thought I saw real potential in a worthless mortal. That was my error. One that I'll be correcting—"

"James, you'll never guess what I found!" Kat burst through the door, dressed in a gauzy nightgown with a pile of clothes draped over her arm. My heart stopped in my chest at the sight of her. I'd been hoping to end this before she ever knew that Teach was still alive. Before I could react, he was behind me. His dagger pressed against my throat.

"Ah, it's the little whore. I'm surprised, James. I would have thought you'd cut her loose after you wet your dick."

"Edward. How…" Katherine's words trailed off; her emerald eyes wide as she took him in.

"How did I survive when you deliberately kept things from me? Is that the question you're burning to ask?" Edward barked at her.

"Please, Edward. Please, just let him go," she pleaded.

"You see that, James. She's begging for your life. Tell me, what lies did you feed her to get her to be so loyal?"

"Fuck you, Teach," I grumbled, his blade digging into my throat.

"Tell me, Katherine, does he fuck you better than I do? Does he know that special spot that makes you scream?"

"Just let him go, Edward. We don't need him anymore. He's served his purpose." Kat's eyes shifted to mine for a moment. Was it sorrow or guilt that I saw reflected back at me? "Don't you see?" she continued. "I needed him to get us to the ruby. All of this was for you. I know where it is." A lump formed in my throat as I tried to decipher her words. What was she saying?

"Don't fuck with me, Katherine. I'm in no mood," Teach warned.

"I couldn't tell you. I had to make it real? Would you have been able to hide it from him if you knew my game?" He paused at that, and I felt him stand straighter as he considered her. "Come over here and let me prove that I'm telling the truth," she said. Something changed in her gaze, a dark truth that she'd never shared with me. My heart broke at her words, and I began to second guess every move I'd made. Every feeling I'd ever had for this woman. Had it all been a façade?

Kat grasped her locket, the one she always wore. "I swear on my mother's locket, I only speak the truth," she said. I watched as she opened the locket, the first time I'd ever seen her open it. She kissed the jewelry reverently in a display of her solidarity. I could feel Teach's grip loosen. His blade fell away from my neck, and he took a step toward Kat. Completely sold on her confession. My mind was having a hard time wrapping around her words. Had I been double crossed? Had our love been one-sided? I couldn't believe it. It was real. I knew it was real.

Teach walked to her, still fidgeting with his blade. He wanted to believe her, but he was skeptical, too. Kat slid her hands up his chest and wrapped her arms around his neck, completely ignoring the blade in his hand. I couldn't pull myself from the spot as my entire world hung in the balance. Katherine reached up on her tiptoes and sealed her lips to his in a passionate kiss.

To Be Continued.

MORE TO COME IN 2024

A

# PENCHANT
### FOR
# POISON

CAPTAIN JAMES HOOK'S STORY
CONTINUES IN PART II OF THIS
NEVERLAND CHRONICLES SAGA

TSKinleyBooks.com

# More From T.S. Kinley
## The Neverland Chronicles

### -Prequel-

### -Volume I-

### -Volume II-

### -Volume III-

TSKinleyBooks.com

# Also Available

# The Smut Diaries

THE SMUT DIARY IS A READING JOURNAL FOR THOSE WHO LIKE IT SPICY. A QUINTESSENTIAL "BLACK BOOK" TO TRACK ALL YOUR BOOK BOYFRIEND AFFAIRS.

TSKinleyBooks.com

# ABOUT THE AUTHOR

T. S. Kinley is a passion project created by two sisters with a shared obsession and vision. We came together with the dream of creating something beautiful, imaginative, and yes... SEXY. *Once Upon a Time...* it all began with sisterly gossip about erotica and romance novels. Our conversations quickly became fantasies about our own desires to author such work. We would muse how some day in a utopian future, our fantasy would become reality. Ultimately we decided rather than wait for the future to find us, we would create utopia ourselves. Using our love of books, natural gift of creativity, and some savvy study on publishing itself, the concept for our very first book was born. We started off as a Cosmetologist and an RN, and quickly developed into a dynamic writing team with a style that lends a unique perspective to our books.

If you haven't signed up already, please subscribe to the T.S. Kinley newsletter.

Receive exclusive sneak peeks on new releases, contests and other spicy content.

Visit www.TSKinleyBooks.com and sign up today!

Follow T.S. Kinley on social media. Let's be friends! Check out our Instagram, Facebook, Pinterest, and Tic Tok pages and get insights into the beautifully, complicated mind of not one, but two authors! You have questions, something you are dying to know about the amazing characters we've created? Join us online, we love to engage with our readers!

AUTHOR

# LIKE WHAT YOU READ?

Did you enjoy your journey into the Neverland Chronicles? Be a love and leave a review on Goodreads. While you are there give us a follow.

Printed in Dunstable, United Kingdom

64242595R00153